# LOVE LETTERS

"I'm going up to visit Adam this weekend," Caroline told Jessica and Lila.

"Good." Lila smiled. "That leaves the next weekend free for him to come here. We're going to throw a party for him."

Caroline gasped. "You don't have to do that, Lila."

"It would be our pleasure," Lila insisted.

Caroline hesitated. "Adam's kind of shy. I don't think he'd like the idea of a party."

"He hardly seems shy in all those letters you've read to us," Jessica said. "And I can't believe you'd turn down the chance to star at your own party."

"I know," Caroline said miserably.

"Great. So it's all set. Tell him in your next letter."

Caroline watched in agony as Jessica and Lila sauntered away. *I've really made a mess of things,* she told herself unhappily. And as far as she could see, there was no way out this time.

Bantam Books in the Sweet Valley High Series
Ask your bookseller for the books you have missed

# SWEET VALLEY HIGH

# LOVE LETTERS

Written by
**Kate William**

Created by
**FRANCINE PASCAL**

**BANTAM BOOKS**
TORONTO • NEW YORK • LONDON • SYDNEY • AUCKLAND

RL6, IL age 12 and up

LOVE LETTERS
*A Bantam Book / March 1985*
*7 printings through April 1987*

*Sweet Valley High is a trademark of Francine Pascal*

*Conceived by Francine Pascal*

*Produced by Cloverdale Press, Inc.*

*Cover art by James Mathewuse*

ISBN 0-553-26883-X

*Published simultaneously in the United States and Canada*

Bantam Books are published by Bantam Books, Inc. Its trademark, consisting of
the words "Bantam Books" and the portrayal of a rooster, is Registered in
U.S. Patent and Trademark Office and in other countries. Marca Registrada.
Bantam Books, Inc., 666 Fifth Avenue, New York, New York 10103.

PRINTED IN THE UNITED STATES OF AMERICA

O    16  15  14  13  12  11  10  9

# LOVE LETTERS

# One

Caroline Pearce sat up in bed and rubbed her eyes sleepily. Late morning sunlight streamed through the blinds on her windows as she stretched lazily, savoring the peace and quiet of Sunday morning. The night before, she thought, had been one of the nicest evenings of her life. And she wanted to stay in bed just a little bit longer, remembering every detail.

The party the Patmans had given the previous night at the exclusive Sweet Valley Country Club was a first for Caroline. It was the first time she felt part of a group, the first time people were friendly to her, the first time, it seemed, that anyone had noticed her at all. But this was only the beginning, she reminded herself, swinging her legs over the side of her bed and running her fingers through her tousled red hair. *Maybe I'll never be as popular as the Wakefield twins or Lila Fowler, but I'm not going to be an outcast anymore. All that has changed now with Adam. Thanks to Adam, people are actually beginning to pay some attention to me.*

It was funny, Caroline thought as she jumped out of bed and hurried over to her dresser. All it seemed to take to get in with the right people was a boyfriend. And an invented boyfriend seemed to work as well as the real thing!

For as long as she could remember, Caroline had wanted to make real friends at Sweet Valley High. She knew as many people as anyone else did—more, in fact. And she made it a point to know what everyone was up to, and who he or she was up to it *with*. According to her older sister, Anita, this made Caroline a gossip. "Telling you a secret is like running an ad in *The Sweet Valley News*," Anita had complained on more than one occasion.

But Caroline didn't think that was one bit fair. "I only try to get in on what's going on because I feel left out," she always defended herself.

"But don't you understand that telling stories about people is the surest way to *stay* left out?" Anita always replied.

It was easy enough for Anita to take that point of view. Anita had everything—looks, boyfriends, good grades. She was doing extremely well in her first year at Sweet Valley College. *I wish she lived on campus instead of at home*, Caroline thought, opening one of her dresser drawers and taking out her bathing suit. It was hard having her at home. Although it was better than the previous year, Caroline reflected. Then, they had both been at Sweet Valley High. *I thought she'd drive me crazy*.

*Yes*, Caroline continued, slipping on the navy-blue tank suit and looking at herself critically in the mirror, *it's all so easy for Anita. She'd probably laugh herself sick if I told her how many times I used to cry myself to sleep when everyone else—including her—was out on dates. Or else she'd say something stupid like 'it doesn't matter,' when it obviously does. She'd tell me I should just be myself, and everything will turn out fine.*

Well, Caroline *had* tried to be herself, and as far as she was concerned, it hadn't worked. Not one little bit. For some reason, boys weren't interested in her.

Even worse, none of the girls in her class seemed very interested in Caroline's company either—at least, not before Adam came along. Now that she had Adam everything had changed. Caroline's face lit up as she remembered the attentive faces the previous night when she'd shown Adam's latest letter to Lila Fowler and Cara Walker at the country club.

She had described Adam with such painstaking precision to everyone at school that she could almost see him before her now. About six feet two, she'd said, with dark brown hair and warm, laughing eyes. She had told everyone that he lived in Cold Springs, a town about two hours' drive from Sweet Valley. He played baseball, and everybody liked him. But what Adam liked best in the whole world was Caroline. That was what his latest letter said, anyway. Caroline had read that letter to so many people she almost believed it had come from a real boyfriend. Almost.

It wasn't her fault, she thought desperately, pulling a hairbrush through her straight red hair. She was sick and tired of being a misfit. And if all it took to be popular was a boyfriend— well, she'd have a boyfriend.

"I *do* have a boyfriend," she whispered aloud, ignoring the hint of sadness she saw in her reflection. "His name is Adam, and he lives in Cold Springs. And he loves me very much."

*That's all I've got to remember*, she told herself, putting on a white oxford-cloth shirt and buttoning her shorts. *One slip-up now, Caroline Pearce, and you're really in trouble.*

But at this point, it was a risk Caroline was all too willing to take.

Anita was reading *The Sweet Valley News* in the breakfast room when Caroline went downstairs. Sweet Valley College was less than five miles from the Pearces' home, and Anita was commuting.

"Do you want a waffle?" Caroline asked cheerfully, popping a frozen one into the toaster for herself and holding the box out to her sister.

"No thanks." Anita yawned. "I'm watching my weight," she added pointedly. Caroline blushed. Anita was model-thin, and Caroline could tell from the insinuating tone in her voice that she was really giving her little sister a hint.

Whenever Caroline complained that Anita was picking on her appearance, her sister looked wide-eyed and innocent. "I'm only trying to help," she'd say. *But I don't have a weight problem*, Caroline reminded herself, fighting to keep her self-control. *And even if I lived on melon and ice water, like Anita does, things wouldn't be any better. I'd be weak and miserable, instead of just miserable. No, Adam is the only hope I've got. And not even Anita is going to wreck how good I'm feeling now that I've got him.*

"You should have seen the club last night," Caroline told her sister, putting her waffle on a plate and joining her at the kitchen table. "It was amazing. The Patmans had centerpieces at every table, big glass bowls filled with water and little candles floating in them, and flowers everywhere! It was gorgeous." She sighed, closing her eyes and remembering.

"It sounds nice," Anita murmured, her eyes glued to the paper.

It was all probably run-of-the-mill to Anita, Caroline thought, sighing. Flowers and candles and country club dances didn't even rate a raised eyebrow. *For once I'd like to tell her something that would really surprise her!*

"Mrs. Patman was wearing the fanciest diamond necklace I've ever seen," Caroline added, smearing her waffle with butter.

Anita lowered her newspaper and glared at the butter as if it were cyanide. "No kidding," she muttered. "Who else was there?"

"Oh, you know," Caroline said vaguely, taking a big bite of waffle. "Everybody. Bruce Patman was with some girl I didn't know, who was wearing the most amazing dress. It was practically see-through!"

Anita went back to her paper.

"And Lila Fowler was wearing a dress from The Designer Shop," Caroline added dreamily. "Cara Walker said it cost over two hundred dollars. She was with a real nerd, though," she added, swallowing a bite of waffle.

"Really?" Anita said dryly, putting the paper down and narrowing her almond-shaped eyes at her younger sister. "And what about you, Caroline? Did you dance with anyone?"

"No," Caroline admitted, her face falling. But it didn't matter, she assured herself quickly. Everyone had believed that Adam couldn't make it because he had a baseball game. They hadn't expected her to dance with anyone else.

"Oh, well," Anita said lightly. "There'll be other dances."

*I hate it when she's so condescending*, Caroline thought furiously. *Just wait till I tell her about Adam. She won't feel sorry for me then!*

"Gosh, I didn't realize it was so late," Caroline said suddenly, catching sight of the clock over the stove. "I'm supposed to meet a bunch of people at the beach."

"Meet who at the beach?" Mrs. Pearce asked, coming into the kitchen and pouring herself a cup of coffee. "Did you have a nice time last night, dear?"

Caroline sighed. Somehow Anita had taken all the joy out of describing the Patmans' party. "It was OK," she mumbled, ignoring the eager expression on her mother's face.

"If you're going to the beach, you can take the car," her mother added helpfully.

"That's OK," Caroline told her. "I'm getting a ride with the Wakefields."

"You are?" Anita's eyebrows shot up in surprise.

Caroline had known that that would interest her sister. Anita thought the Wakefields were the nicest girls in Caroline's class. She was always pushing Caroline to get to know the twins better.

"Sure," Caroline said airily. "We set the whole thing up last night." Actually Caroline had overheard Cara offering Jessica a ride. And only her newfound confidence, now that Jessica knew about Adam, had prompted Caroline to ask if she could go along. Jessica had looked noncommittal, but Caroline thought she'd walk over to the Wakefields' anyway to see what the twins were up to. *Things are different now*, she reminded herself stubbornly. *Everyone thinks I have a boyfriend, and that's all I need to fit in.*

*If only there really were someone named Adam*, Caroline thought wistfully, hurrying upstairs to get her beach things. Someone who really looked forward to seeing her, who wrote her letters and called her on the phone—someone she could talk to, when she was worried about things at school or at home. . . .

For just a minute, stepping inside her bedroom, Caroline's eyes blurred with tears. She

8

brushed them away impatiently, but not before she'd had time to think that she had other reasons for wanting a boyfriend besides just impressing people.

The truth of the matter was that Caroline Pearce was lonely.

"You get it, Liz," Jessica Wakefield begged, hearing the door bell peal below. "It's Caroline Pearce," she hissed, her sun-streaked blond hair streaming as she flew unobserved from her perch at Elizabeth's window.

Elizabeth sighed, putting down the pad of paper she'd been writing on. "Jess, I'm busy," she complained, sensing defeat even as she spoke. It never failed to amaze Elizabeth how good her twin sister was at giving her all the dirty work.

Sixteen years old, blond-haired, with blue-green eyes, the twins were identical, down to the gold lavalieres they wore around their necks—birthday presents from their parents. They were both five feet six, with model-slim, size-six figures. But there the resemblance ended. Jessica was as tempestuous as Elizabeth was calm. Jessica threw herself with astounding energy into every new plan or relationship, more often than not getting herself into scrapes. And Elizabeth, whose rational side usually kept her out of trouble, was often obliged to come to her rescue.

"Come on," Jessica prompted now, her blue-green eyes sparkling. "You're so much more diplomatic than I am."

"I think it's mean," Elizabeth declared, striding across the room as the door bell rang again. "If you're going to the beach, why can't you let her come along?"

"Cara and I have private things to discuss," Jessica said. "Come on, Liz. You know what a pain Caroline is."

"What am I supposed to tell her?" Elizabeth demanded from the top of the short stairway in their split-level house.

"You're the one who's so creative," Jessica reminded her. "Just use your imagination. And hurry—Cara's picking me up any second."

Elizabeth shook her head, quickening her steps as the door bell rang again. Her parents were both working that day—unusual for a Sunday—but Ned Wakefield was busy with a case that would be in court the next week, and Alice Wakefield was showing a design to a client who could come to town only that day. *And I thought I'd have peace and quiet this morning to work on my play*, Elizabeth thought.

"Hi, Caroline," Elizabeth said, opening the

10

front door and giving the redhead a smile. "How are you?"

"I was wondering if you and Jessica were going to the beach," Caroline asked shyly, her pale skin turning pink under the spatter of freckles across her nose and cheeks.

Elizabeth looked ruefully at the cloudless sky and shook her head. "I can't," she said. "I've got some work to do."

"Oh, come on," Caroline said, looking more confident. "It's too nice outside to work. Besides, you always get straight A's."

Elizabeth flushed. "This isn't schoolwork," she told her. "I'm working on a one-act play for the Junior Playwriting Contest. And I don't have much time to get it all researched and written."

"I'm sure you'll win, no matter what," Caroline assured her. "I'll bet no one else will even enter."

Elizabeth glanced quizzically at her, her brow wrinkling. *There's a left-handed compliment!* she thought to herself. "Actually," she said, "Bill Chase is submitting a play, too. He's gotten really interested in drama ever since Mr. Gordon discovered him, and his play is supposed to be really good." Mr. Gordon was an influential talent agent, and the father of Bill's girlfriend, DeeDee.

"I'm sure it isn't," Caroline insisted. She

11

blushed, staring down at the ground. "I mean, I'm sure yours is better."

Elizabeth smiled at her, not certain what to say. It seemed that Caroline was trying to be nice, but somehow things kept coming out wrong.

"Todd will be there, won't he?" Caroline continued, a wheedling note coming into her voice.

Elizabeth was beginning to get irritated. She didn't know whether or not Todd was going to the beach, but she didn't like the way Caroline made it sound. Caroline seemed to assume she'd leap at the chance to go along if Todd would be around. Elizabeth and Todd Wilkins had been a couple for a long time, but they didn't need to spend every minute together. Todd knew her well enough to know how much this competition meant to her. Elizabeth had worked on *The Oracle*, Sweet Valley High's newspaper, for two years now. She was an experienced writer, but this play was her first creative piece to be judged by others.

"I really can't come, Caroline," she repeated firmly. "But thanks for asking."

"What about Jessica?" Caroline asked, looking past Elizabeth into the Wakefields' foyer.

"Jessica—" Elizabeth thought for a minute.

"Jessica's sleeping," she said at last. "She probably won't be up for ages."

"Oh," Caroline said, her face falling. "Maybe I could come inside and wait for her," she suggested hopefully.

For just a minute Elizabeth toyed with the idea of inviting Caroline in and trapping her twin upstairs. But despite her irritation with Caroline, Elizabeth felt genuinely sorry for her. There was no point in giving her false hope. And Jessica would probably climb out the window if Caroline came inside, anyway.

"I don't think that's a good idea," Elizabeth told her. "You know Jess. She's probably going to be in bed till about one o'clock. Why don't you go on ahead? Jessica will follow eventually."

"OK," Caroline said slowly, twisting nervously at her hair. "I guess I'll just take the bus, then."

"Have a good time," Elizabeth said as she closed the door.

Caroline headed listlessly down the walk. *I will have a good time*, Caroline thought. *There's bound to be a few people around to talk to. And I'm not going to let the Wakefields spoil my mood.* She stopped at the end of the walk to retie the laces on her tennis shoes.

A neighborhood dog had knocked the lid off the trash can the Wakefields had set out neatly by the side of the road, and Caroline picked the lid up, leaning over to fit it back in place. As she did so, a sheet of paper caught her eye. It was a dark photocopy of a letter addressed to a company in San Francisco, and it was signed by Alice Wakefield.

Caroline hesitated to read the letter, but curiosity had always been one of her strongest traits. She read the photocopy quickly as she walked to the bus stop, becoming more and more amazed with each successive line. "I don't believe this," she muttered to herself at last, folding the letter neatly and tucking it into her bag. She smiled. *I don't look for gossip, it looks for me.* And this latest piece of news was the most explosive to have found Caroline yet.

# Two

"I still can't believe this," Lila Fowler muttered, tossing her copy of *Ingenue* magazine into the sand. "I can't for the life of me imagine what that modeling agency saw in Regina Morrow. I think she looks kind of cross-eyed," she added, studying the cover from a new angle.

Jessica snorted, turning over and letting the sun bake the backs of her slender legs. "That's not a trace of envy I notice, is it?" she asked. Jessica couldn't resist teasing Lila about Regina. Before Regina had moved to Sweet Valley, Lila had been the richest girl in town. It was bad enough that Regina was also rich, but she was friendly, outgoing, and devastatingly beautiful, which hadn't made Lila feel very friendly toward her.

"I'm not the slightest bit jealous of Regina Morrow!" Lila burst out indignantly. "I think modeling is vulgar," she added after a moment. She was glad nobody knew she had gone to the modeling agency hoping to persuade the head of the agency to use *her* on the cover of the magazine. It was bad enough as it was, Lila thought glumly. Regina was getting so much attention it was sickening.

"I can feel my brain cells collapsing in this heat." Cara Walker moaned and rolled over on her back.

Jessica giggled. "That shouldn't take too long," she teased her friend, giving Cara a sand shower.

"Don't look now," Lila said suddenly, "but Caroline Pearce is approaching."

"Ambush!" Jessica shrieked, grabbing a towel as if to hide under it.

"Shut up, Jess. She's heading in this direction," Cara warned her, sitting up and shading her eyes with one hand.

Actually Caroline was uncertain about what she was doing. She had arrived at the beach about two hours earlier, hoping to see someone she knew. The beach was packed with people sitting in pairs or threesomes on beach towels, but Caroline hadn't spotted anyone from Sweet Valley High. She had always loved the ocean, so she decided to stay anyway. But now she was beginning to get bored. Ready to leave, she had put on her shorts and shirt, then decided to look around once more for someone she recognized.

Suddenly Caroline caught sight of Jessica, sitting with Cara and Lila about a dozen yards from the lifeguard's chair. *Thank goodness*, she thought happily, threading her way over to them between the beach towels. *It would be awful to spend an afternoon like this alone!*

"I'm so glad I found you guys," she said breathlessly, putting her towel down next to Jessica's. "I stopped over at your house earlier," she said to Jessica, "but your sister said you were still asleep, so I took the bus. I can't believe how mobbed this place is."

"Not mobbed enough." Lila yawned, covering her mouth with a perfectly manicured hand.

"What?" Caroline asked, looking confused.

"Lila's just looking for more boys," Jessica said.

Caroline sank down on her towel and struggled out of her shorts and shirt. *I wish I could look like Jessica in that bikini,* she thought wistfully. A quick glance down at her old tank suit confirmed her fears.

Jessica and Lila had resumed their conversation, and Caroline sat quietly listening, wishing she had something to contribute. She wanted so badly to belong to their group, to say something that might interest them!

"I don't suppose any of you heard about Annie Whitman and Ricky Capaldo?" she asked suddenly when a break came in the conversation. Nobody said anything. Lila yawned loudly, and Jessica turned over again, looking critically at the skin on her shoulders.

"Annie was pretty angry with him last night," Caroline tried again.

"Really?" Cara said, not sounding very interested.

"I'm sure you all noticed that she and Ricky stormed off the dance floor at the club," Caroline said uncertainly, taking a deep breath. "Well, the way I heard it, Ricky had promised Annie that he'd take her to the party in his father's Cadillac. It's a white Seville, I think. And Annie was thrilled. But at the last minute his father changed his mind and Ricky picked her up in his old beat-up Chevy. And Annie got shrimp cocktail sauce all over her dress, and when she came back from the ladies' lounge after she tried to get it off, she saw Ricky talking to Maria Santelli. He came up with some sort of feeble excuse, but Annie knew better because it's happened before. That's what she told someone, anyway. And then the next time they danced together, Ricky stepped on Annie's foot. She was wearing sandals, and she thought her foot was practically *broken* and everything, and she called her mother to come pick her up. She said she wouldn't leave with Ricky for anything in the whole world."

"Hmmm," Cara mused. "Well, I guess that means Ricky Capaldo is available."

"Are you kidding, Cara?" Jessica said. "He's not your type at all."

"But he *is* a guy," Cara reasoned. "And sometimes I feel I can't be that choosy."

"There's always Winston," Jessica offered, giggling.

"He's OK for a laugh," Cara said, snickering. "But I can't stand guys who are thinner than I am."

Jessica and Lila both laughed, but Caroline felt her stomach tighten. She didn't see what was so funny about Winston Egbert. Unlike the others, she'd once had a crush on the gangly class clown, though he'd never paid any attention to her.

Lila turned over on her back. "John Pfeifer's not so bad."

"Sure, if you're a football," Cara grumbled. "He's so into being Mr. Ace Sports Editor, he probably doesn't have time for girls."

"I don't know," Jessica said. "Liz spends as much time on *The Oracle* as John does, and take my word for it, she has plenty of time for Todd."

"But John's strictly a sidelines guy," Cara continued. "He likes to watch the action, not get involved."

Caroline had been listening eagerly to the conversation, hoping she'd be able to contribute something again. "I wouldn't depend much on John," she told them seriously. "I have a feeling he's going to be off girls for a while. He and Penny had a huge fight Friday afternoon, and he may be kicked off the newspaper for good." Penny Ayala was *The Oracle*'s editor in chief.

The others stared at her. "I don't believe it," Jessica said suddenly, her expression darkening. "Liz didn't say anything about it. And if anyone knows what's going on at *The Oracle*, she does."

"It's true," Caroline insisted. "I heard something about his sports copy being late all the time."

Cara let a handful of sand slip through her fingers. "It's just like I was telling you, Jess. We're running short of guys around here."

"I don't know," Caroline said softly. "I used to feel the same way, Cara. But if you take your time and wait for the right guy, it makes everything worthwhile."

Lila and Jessica exchanged glances. "Are you

20

talking about that guy you met in Old Springs?" Lila demanded, suddenly looking interested. "What's his name again?"

"Adam," Caroline said dreamily. "And it's *Cold* Springs," she corrected her. "He called me this morning," she added, looking shyly at the sand.

"That was an amazing letter he sent you," Cara said. "It was so poetic—your souls floating together and him loving you more after you're dead."

"He's terribly romantic," Caroline admitted. "You should have heard him on the phone today! He made me tell him that I love him, even though my mother was right in the next room!"

"Did you?" Jessica asked, arching her eyebrows.

"Of course," Caroline told her. "How could I help it? There's something so—so commanding about him. It was impossible not to fall in love with him. And he's in love with me, too," she added, ignoring the look Cara was giving Lila. "He says he's counting the hours until he sees me again."

"When do you suppose that will be?" Lila asked.

Caroline flushed. She didn't like the turn the conversation was taking. It was one thing to fill everyone in on all the romantic details, but the practical details were another matter altogether. "He didn't mean *hours* in the literal sense," she said evasively. "He doesn't use language the way most guys do. I told you, he's very poetic."

"But that doesn't answer my question," Lila pointed out. "When—"

"Oh, look," Caroline interrupted, jumping to her feet and showering Jessica with sand. "There's Maria down by the water. If you three will excuse me, I'm going to ask her what's going on with Ricky and Annie. I'll be back in a minute."

"Lucky us," Jessica muttered, brushing sand off her shoulders. "That girl is amazingly clumsy," she added, squinting at Caroline's shrinking figure in the bright sunlight.

"I don't know where she got that bathing suit." Cara giggled. "It looks like something you'd wear for gym class!"

Lila nodded. "She sure didn't meet this Adam guy at the beach," she agreed. "Though where she *did* meet him is a good question. He must have a few screws loose if he's serious about Caroline."

"Maybe he's nearsighted," Cara said.

"He'd have to be nearsighted *and* hard of hearing to tolerate even five minutes with her," Jessica pointed out. "It's her voice that drives me crazy. No wonder they have to depend on letters!"

"Do your imitation of her, Jess," Cara begged.

Jessica laughed, jumping to her feet. "Oh, look, there's Maria down by the water," she said in a high, irritating falsetto. "If you three will *just* excuse me, I'll be *right* back."

Lila was gesturing furiously at Jessica to stop, but Jessica paid no attention.

"That's pretty good, Jess," Caroline said uncomfortably, coming up behind her. "Is that what I sound like?"

Jessica spun around to face the redhead. "Not really," she told her. "We're just being silly."

"What did Maria have to say?" Cara asked, trying to save Jessica from embarrassment by changing the subject.

Caroline shrugged. "She said she didn't know what was going on."

"In other words, she told you to mind your own business," Jessica remarked.

Caroline's face burned. She had tried to play along with Jessica, but she'd had about all she could take of this. "I guess that would be your advice, wouldn't it, Jessica?" she asked archly. "But then in your predicament you've got enough to worry about without thinking about other people."

"And what predicament is that?" Jessica demanded lightly.

"Well," Caroline began, her eyes sparkling with anger, "you must be awfully busy getting ready to move. Sixteen years is a long time in one place," she went on, "and it must be hard to tear yourself away from Sweet Valley. I understand, Jess."

"What are you talking about?" Jessica laughed. "I'm not going anywhere."

"Are you going to stay behind when your whole family moves?" Caroline asked, looking shocked.

Jessica paled. "Is this some kind of joke?" she asked, her eyes beginning to spark with anger.

"Not unless *this* is a joke," Caroline retorted, plucking the photocopied letter she'd found that morning out of her bag and handing it to Jessica.

Jessica sat down, unfolded the letter, and read it quickly, her jaw dropping open in disbelief. The letter was from her mother, written to a large design firm in San Francisco. In the letter Mrs. Wakefield thanked them for their job offer and said she had to think it over, though the position looked too attractive to turn down. She'd be back in touch soon, but in any case she wouldn't be able to move her whole family to a new city for at least a month.

*A month!* Jessica thought, her head spinning.

What in the world was going on? Why hadn't her mother said anything to her or Elizabeth?

"Jess, what's going on?" Cara asked impatiently, grabbing her arm. "You're not really moving, are you?"

"Of course not," Jessica scoffed, glaring at Caroline. "Mom told Liz and me about this *weeks* ago," she added, fighting to control her voice. "It's no big deal," she added airily. "She's just stringing them along. You guys can't get rid of me *that* easily," she assured them.

"Well, I guess I'd better be going," Caroline said, putting on her shirt. She knew she wasn't going to get any more of a reaction from Jessica, although she sensed the letter was a bigger surprise than Jessica would ever admit. "I have to write a letter to Adam," Caroline added, buttoning her shorts and picking up her beach bag.

Cara and Lila murmured something about seeing her later, but Jessica barely heard them. Her mind was racing. The letter Caroline had given her had shocked her, and the only thing she could think of was getting home and confronting her parents. "What time is it?" she asked.

"I don't know," Cara said. "Around two-thirty, I guess."

"God, I completely forgot!" Jessica gasped,

smacking her forehead and doing her best to look as if she'd just remembered something crucial. "I was supposed to get home and help Liz with something about ten minutes ago. I'd better go," she told them, hastily gathering her things together. "You guys stay. I can take the bus."

Cara turned to Lila. "I've about had it with this place. Nothing's happening. Why don't we leave now and drop Jessica off, then go and get something to eat?"

"Great idea," Lila responded.

"Thanks, Cara," Jessica said gratefully. The sooner she got home the better. *Because even as it is*, she thought as she waited for Cara and Lila to gather up their things, *I have a feeling I may be too late. From the sound of that letter, Mom's already made her mind up for all of us.*

But that, Jessica thought, was a fate too horrible to consider.

# Three

The Wakefields' attractive, split-level home was quiet when Jessica let herself in. "I'm home!" she yelled, throwing her beach bag near the staircase and heading toward the Spanish-tiled kitchen her mother had lovingly designed a few years back. But no one answered.

A note propped up on the kitchen counter explained the Sunday afternoon quiet. It was from Elizabeth, who had taken a break from working on her play and had gone over to Todd's. "Mom and Dad are picking up pizza for dinner and will be back around six o'clock," the note explained.

Jessica sniffed forlornly. *It figures*, she thought, walking slowly up the stairs to her bedroom and throwing herself down on her unmade bed. Her parents had quite clearly forgotten that she and Elizabeth existed. They'd both turned into workaholics. They didn't care that they were about to destroy their daughters' lives.

Overcome with sadness, Jessica looked around her room. "It's taken forever to get this room looking like this!" she wailed.

"I'll bet it has," her twin said wryly, poking her head into the room.

"Liz!" Jessica shrieked, leaping off her bed and engulfing her sister in a warm hug. "Where have you *been*?"

Elizabeth laughed, untangling her sister's arms. "I just got back from Todd's. What's wrong?" she asked suddenly, getting a closer look at Jessica's face. "You're not afraid someone's going to destroy your decor, are you?"

Ordinarily Jessica would have laughed. Her room was a source of jokes in the Wakefield household, and Elizabeth was the one who got the most mileage out of it. Jessica didn't care what anyone said. She liked it just the way it was. She had painted the walls dark brown— "Like a mud pit," Elizabeth said—and she left it, as she said, "au naturel." Elizabeth said that meant throwing clothes on the floor instead of hanging them up.

None of this made Jessica feel any better right now. The thought of leaving this room, of leaving Sweet Valley, brought stormy tears to her blue-green eyes. "Liz, look at this," she said, taking out the crumpled letter Caroline had given her.

Elizabeth took the letter from her, smoothing it out and scanning the typed page with worried eyes. "Where did you get this, Jess?" she whispered when she'd finished reading.

Jessica flung herself dramatically on her bed. "Caroline Pearce, homewrecker and busybody. I shudder to think where *she* got it. But the point is, Liz—what are we going to *do*?"

Elizabeth sighed and sat down on the edge of her sister's bed. The expression on her pretty face mirrored Jessica's. A mixture of confusion, hurt, and panic flashed in her blue-green eyes. "Well," she said at last, trying to keep her voice calm, "we'll just have to talk it out with Mom and Dad. Mom didn't say she'd reached a final decision," she reminded Jessica. "We'll just have to try our hardest to be reasonable with them."

"Reasonable!" Jessica wailed. "Liz, how can you talk like that? Don't you realize we're doomed? Finished? Completely ruined?"

Elizabeth laughed. "Take it easy, Jess," she warned. "That's not the way to change anyone's mind—or to help persuade anyone who isn't completely convinced yet. We've *got* to be calm about this."

"OK," Jessica said meekly. "I'll be calm, Liz—I promise."

But when it came to moving away from Sweet Valley, Jessica Wakefield didn't know the meaning of the word calm. Her parents had barely taken the pizza out of its cardboard box when the first explosion occurred. Alice Wakefield, her blond hair tied back neatly in a ponytail, was taking plates out of the cupboard when Jessica stormed downstairs. Usually the sight of her mother's youthful, blue-eyed face brought a smile to Jessica's face. But that night Jessica looked stormy and sullen.

"Is something wrong, Jess?" Ned Wakefield asked.

Jessica's lower lip quivered as she sat down at the table. She tried to remain in control but couldn't. Finally the dam burst. "Mom, how could you *do* this to us?" she wailed.

Mrs. Wakefield laughed as she put the plates on the table, then sat down. "I take it you're not in the mood for pizza, Jess."

Elizabeth, who had just entered the room, shot her twin a warning look, but it was too late. Tears spilling down her cheeks, Jessica looked angrily from her father to her mother.

"Who cares about pizza?" she demanded. "I'm talking about my whole *life*!"

"Jessica," Ned Wakefield said mildly, leaning back in his chair, "would you mind telling us what this is all about?"

"*This* is what I'm talking about." Jessica took the letter from the breast pocket of her shirt and handed it to her mother. "Mom, how could you do this to us? Don't Liz and I even get to know when we're about to be completely uprooted?"

Alice Wakefield stared down at the letter for a moment without speaking. "Where did you find this, Jess?" she finally asked.

"A friend gave it to me," Jessica told her. Realizing how lame that sounded, she shook her blond head furiously. "It doesn't matter where I found it," she insisted. "The thing I don't understand is why you didn't tell us about it ages ago!"

Mrs. Wakefield sighed and looked imploringly at her husband. "I didn't know about it ages ago, that's why," she told Jessica. "A little over a week ago I got a call from John Paine, the director of the Hurley Group. I'm sure you two have heard me mention them before. They're one of the biggest design firms in the state, and Mr. Paine wants me to head up one of their departments. It's a very flattering offer," she pointed out. "I didn't tell you two last week

31

because I wanted some time to think about it first and to talk it over with your father."

"But now I suppose your mind is made up," Jessica snapped.

"Jessica," Mr. Wakefield said sternly, "I don't like your tone. Don't you think you ought to congratulate your mother?"

Jessica stared down at her plate.

"We're both proud of you, Mom," Elizabeth said slowly. "I guess it's just kind of a shock."

"I know." Mrs. Wakefield sighed. "It's a shock to all of us. And we'll all have to think about it and talk about it before we make up our minds. But—"

"How can you even consider it?" Jessica shrieked. "You've lived in Sweet Valley all your lives. How can you even think about leaving?"

"That's part of our consideration, Jess," Mr. Wakefield pointed out. "It might be nice to have a change. After all, San Francisco is a beautiful city. I've always really liked it there. And I'm sure you two—"

"But, Dad." Now Elizabeth interrupted, forgetting all about her promise to stay calm. "What about your practice? You wouldn't give up law, would you?"

Mr. Wakefield laughed. "Not exactly," he told her. "I'd just look for a new firm, Liz. In fact

I've already spoken to a few firms up north that could use an experienced partner."

Elizabeth paled. It looked as if her parents really were serious about this move. Everything had been considered and talked out—everything, that is, but Jessica and Elizabeth. What in the world would *they* do in San Francisco?

"I don't suppose," Jessica pointed out, "that you two have thought about how *we'd* feel about moving?"

Mrs. Wakefield sighed. "Of course we have," she told her daughter. "Believe me, it's one of our biggest worries. I know how hard it would be for you two to leave in the middle of high school, but—"

"*Hard!*" Jessica shrieked. "That's an understatement," she added bitterly. "Mom, it'd be bad enough for *me*. I'd have to give up everything—cheerleading, all my friends, you name it. But think about Liz! How can you possibly expect her to just take off and leave Todd!"

"Girls, I know how hard it would be for you both," Mrs. Wakefield said wearily. "And believe me, we're not going to rush into this thing. But—"

"But basically you've already made up your minds," Jessica cried. "You're just too selfish to listen to what we're saying."

"OK, that's enough," Mr. Wakefield said

angrily, throwing his napkin down on the table. "Jessica, *you're* the one who's being too selfish to listen. Your mother has worked for a long time to reach this step in her career, and I'm disappointed in both of you for not appreciating what an opportunity this is for her. We have *not* made up our minds, and we don't intend to do so without considering your feelings very carefully. But right now I think you both owe your mother a little more consideration."

Jessica began to sob. "I just can't bear it. When I think of having to say goodbye to Lila and Cara . . ."

"That's it," Mr. Wakefield said furiously. "Jessica, I want you to excuse yourself and go up to your room until you're capable of talking this over like an adult."

"I was just leaving anyway!" Jessica leaped to her feet. She tossed her napkin on the table and charged upstairs, her footsteps making the whole house shake.

Elizabeth looked from one parent's distraught face to the other's. "If you'll excuse me, I'm going upstairs, too," she murmured, folding her napkin neatly and hurrying upstairs after her twin. For once Elizabeth didn't blame Jessica for making a scene. The way she was feeling, it hardly seemed to matter.

But as soon as she'd left the room, Elizabeth's anger began to wane. *Dad's right*, she thought. *We weren't very excited for Mom, and this offer is obviously important to her.*

The thought of leaving Sweet Valley was almost too distressing for Elizabeth to consider. She loved everything about the town and couldn't imagine leaving it.

But Elizabeth had a feeling that the way to convince her parents to stay wasn't to cry and beg them to change their minds. "We've got to come up with a plan," she said softly to herself, pausing at the top of the landing and tapping gently on Jessica's door.

"Come in." Jessica lifted her tear-streaked face as Elizabeth opened her door.

"Jessica Wakefield," Elizabeth said, a mischievous sparkle in her turquoise eyes, "I think it's time for you and me to come up with a little scheme."

"What are you talking about, Liz?" Jessica sighed. "Our scheming days are over. All that's ahead of us is packing our bags and getting dragged to a new city. I can hear the streetcars already."

"It isn't like you to give up so easily," Elizabeth pointed out. "I think we went about it all wrong tonight," she added. "From now on,

35

we've got to put our heads together and stick to a plan!"

"What plan?" Jessica demanded, wiping her eyes and looking interested at last.

"Well, that's the problem," Elizabeth admitted. "There isn't one yet. But there will be soon!" she said quickly, before Jessica could start sobbing again. "And it's up to you and me to devise it!"

Elizabeth stared down at her note pad a few hours later, her head spinning. The lines she'd written earlier now took on a whole new meaning, and despite herself, tears welled up in her eyes.

Elizabeth had gotten the inspiration for her play from Olivia Davidson, the arts editor of *The Oracle*. Olivia hadn't exactly given her the idea, but she had loaned Elizabeth the book that had sparked her interest in Elizabeth Barrett Browning. It was a slim volume of poetry called *Sonnets from the Portuguese*, and Elizabeth had been so moved by the beautiful love poems that she'd decided to find out more about the author. That was when she'd learned about the romance between Elizabeth Barrett and the man who became her husband, poet Robert Browning. Elizabeth Barrett had been an invalid most of her adult life, but that hadn't prevented her from falling in love with Browning or from marrying him.

Filled with letters Browning had written referring to loss and separation, the play moved Elizabeth to tears now. She couldn't help noticing the irony in the lines. When she'd begun the play, she'd had no idea that she and Todd might be separated. Now the words took on special meaning for her. She couldn't bear the thought of having to leave Todd. *But he's not going to know about it for now,* she vowed. *There must be some way Jessica and I can convince Mom and Dad to stay. And I don't want to burden Todd with the news before it's final.*

When the door bell rang downstairs, Elizabeth was jolted back to reality. She had forgotten that Todd was coming over. She glanced at her alarm clock. They were supposed to meet Olivia Davidson and Roger Patman at the Dairi Burger in ten minutes, and Elizabeth hadn't even gotten dressed!

Quick as a flash she washed her face and slipped on a fresh cotton T-shirt, brushed her blond hair until it shone, and pulled it into a simple ponytail. Todd was talking to her parents downstairs, and she wanted to hurry so they wouldn't have time to mention San Francisco to him.

But she needn't have worried. Her parents had confined themselves to small talk, and Todd was in high spirits as they drove to the Dairi Burger. "What's wrong?" he asked at last, noticing her silence.

Elizabeth sighed. "I guess I'm just worried about my play," she fibbed. "I've still got so much work to do on it, and I don't have much time left." *Especially if I have to spend all my time worrying about how to keep the family in Sweet Valley*, she added silently.

"I'm sure your play will be terrific," Todd said loyally. "When do I get to read it?"

"As soon as it's done," Elizabeth promised. "I don't know, Todd," she added, looking sadly up at his handsome face as he parked the car in the lot next to the Dairi Burger. "I have a feeling Bill Chase may be writing something really good. He's learned so much about drama since he met DeeDee's father."

A couple of months earlier, before he had a role in Sweet Valley High's junior-class play, Bill Chase wasn't interested in anything but surfing. But on opening night, he had been discovered by DeeDee's father, an agent, who signed Bill up and sent him to Hollywood to film a screen test. Although Bill hadn't become a star overnight, he did have dreams of becoming a professional actor.

"Your play will be better," Todd insisted, his brown eyes twinkling. "Hey," he added lightly, "don't look so down!"

"I'm sorry," Elizabeth said, trying hard to smile. "I guess I'm just getting too wrapped up in this whole thing." Slipping her arm around Todd, she followed him into the Dairi Burger.

"There's Roger," Todd said, taking her hand and leading her to a table in the corner.

"Hi!" Roger Patman called, waving at them. "Olivia's getting us some food," he added, pointing to the counter where the slim, frizzy-haired girl was balancing four milk shakes on a tray.

"Hi, Liz! How's the play going?" Olivia asked, setting the tray down on the table.

Elizabeth shrugged. "I don't know," she said noncommittally. It was harder than she'd realized to try to act as if nothing were wrong. Looking around the Dairi Burger, Elizabeth saw the faces of the kids she'd grown up with, and her eyes blurred with tears. How could she possibly leave Sweet Valley? Above all, how could she ever leave Todd? She grabbed his hand suddenly and squeezed it as hard as she could.

Olivia looked away for a moment, then turned back. "Uh-oh," she said. "Looks like trouble's approaching!"

"What do you mean?" Todd asked curiously, squeezing Elizabeth's hand back under the table.

"Caroline Pearce." Olivia sighed and took a sip of her milk shake. "Don't turn around," she warned him. "She's coming over here, and it looks like she's got something on her mind."

"Liz, I'm so glad to see you!" Caroline said, pulling a chair up to the table and sitting down. "I want you to apologize to Jessica for me," she said.

"What for?" Elizabeth asked warily, a sinking sensation in her stomach signaling that trouble was coming.

"I should never have brought up your mother's plans in front of Jessica's friends," Caroline admitted, oblivious to the attentive expressions on the other faces at the table. "It wasn't fair."

"That's OK, Caroline," Elizabeth said reluctantly.

"What plans?" Todd asked.

Caroline looked slowly around the table, the light dawning in her green eyes. "Oh, no!" she gasped, smacking her forehead with her hand. "Oh, Liz, I've put my foot in my mouth again!"

"Why?" Todd asked curiously. "Liz, what's she talking about?"

Elizabeth sighed, pushed her milk shake away and took a deep breath. "Todd, there's something I've got to tell you," she began slowly. "I didn't want to worry you before the plans were final, but it looks as if now's as good a time as any to break the bad news."

# Four

Monday afternoon after school Jessica breezed into her father's law office. "Hi, Mrs. Kelly," she greeted the receptionist. "Where's my father?"

"In his office. Go right in." The attractive, gray-haired woman waved down the hall in the general direction of Mr. Wakefield's office before answering a phone call.

Ned Wakefield was sitting behind the antique mahogany desk in his large, comfortable corner office, jotting down some notes for a brief he planned to file in court later that week.

Jessica strode purposefully into the room without even knocking. "Hi, Daddy," she said. She ran over and kissed him on the cheek before he could respond. "I had to go to Dr. Perkins's, and since I was in the area I decided to drop by and surprise you. I'm not interrupting anything important, am I?" Her blue-green eyes pleaded with him to say no.

Her effort was unnecessary. Mr. Wakefield returned the kiss with a smile. "I've always got time for a daughter," he said warmly. "I didn't know you had a checkup today."

"Oh, I didn't. I just had to get a form signed, some health thing they require for cheerleading. Nothing important." The fib rolled easily off her tongue. Jessica knew her father wouldn't bother checking it out. Casually she picked up one of the papers on his desk. "What's this?" she asked.

"A divorce petition. No one you know," he added quickly. Then he grimaced. "It's going to be a messy one."

"Who are you representing? The husband or the wife?" Jessica asked.

"The wife."

Jessica walked away from the desk and leaned against a case of legal books. "I guess it's going to be hard to represent her from San Francisco," she said slyly, pouting prettily at her father.

But if she'd expected sympathy from her father, he wasn't prepared to offer it. "So that's what this visit is really about. I should have figured that out when you walked in. You're still upset about last night."

"You bet I am," Jessica cried. "How you and Mom could even think of leaving Sweet Valley is beyond me."

"This job offer opens up a lot of new possibilities for your mother—a bigger salary, more prestigious clients, more challenging projects. An offer like that's not so easy to refuse."

"So what are you supposed to do, Daddy? You've got a wonderful job here. Do you mean to tell me you're willing to chuck it all just like that?"

Mr. Wakefield shook his head. "I'll be honest with you, Jess. Sure, I'd be making a sacrifice. It wouldn't be easy. But I could end up doing better in San Francisco. I've begun to put out a few feelers and—"

"And you're ready to start packing your bags. I suppose I'll come home from school tomorrow and find a moving van outside the house." Jessica's lower lip began to tremble, but this time she wasn't acting.

Mr. Wakefield rose from his chair to calm his daughter. He put his arm around her shoulders and led her to one of the wing chairs next to his desk. He sat down on the other. "Jessica, your mother and I realize that a move would be

44

tough for you and Elizabeth, and believe me, we're considering your feelings in this."

"So why didn't you tell us about it sooner? Why did I have to find out from—well, almost from a perfect stranger!" Tears were beginning to well up in her eyes.

"Try not to be so hard on us—especially your mother," Mr. Wakefield said. "She didn't want to tell you until she'd made up her mind. She didn't want to upset you needlessly."

"Well, she has!"

"I know, and I'm sorry. But you and Liz have got to understand. If we move it will be because of you and Liz, in a way. It won't be long before you'll be going off to college, and with tuition costs being what they are—well, a move like this begins to make sense."

"But what if I don't want to go to college? Maybe I'll just stay here and get a job."

"Jessica, that's enough!" Mr. Wakefield stood up. "Now go home and forget any ideas you have about giving your mother a hard time. She deserves to take this job, and the only reason she hasn't said yes is because of you and Liz. She's made a lot of sacrifices for you girls and your brother over the years. The least I expect from you now is to respect her right to get what she deserves out of life. Do you read me?" His dark eyes bore down on hers.

"Yes, Daddy," Jessica said quietly. She knew when she'd overdone it. And her father had clearly had enough for one day. She got up from the chair.

"That's my girl," Mr. Wakefield said, patting her shoulder. "I'll see you at home."

Jessica stormed out of the office without saying goodbye to Mrs. Kelly or to any of the other office staff she'd known practically forever. As she walked to the elevator banks, she thought briefly about how strange it would be to visit her father in a new office where he'd be surrounded by strangers.

Her thoughts were interrupted by the sound of a familiar voice. "Hi, Jess. It's so good to see you again."

Jessica turned around and found herself face to face with Dennis Creighton.

"Oh, hi, Dennis," she said casually, pushing the down button on the elevator. There was a time when Jessica would have gone out of her mind at the thought of a few minutes alone with Dennis, who helped out at his father's advertising agency across the hall from Mr. Wakefield's office. In fact, she'd put a lot of long hard hours in at her father's office after school, helping with office work, just for a chance to get to know the good-looking boy better. But that was before Jessica had found out that Dennis was only fifteen. Fifteen! As if she would ever dream of going out with a younger guy!

"What brings you to the office on a day like today?" he asked her, leaning against the wall and smiling at her.

Jessica shrugged. "Nothing special," she said airily. She didn't have time for him. Especially not now, she thought. If her days in Sweet Valley were numbered, she didn't feel like wasting them in the sandbox!

"See you later," she murmured to Dennis, brushing past him into the empty elevator. She didn't even notice his disappointed expression . When Jessica Wakefield had something on her mind, she was hard to distract. And right then the one thing that concerned her was the threat of her parents' move. *Liz is right*, she thought as the elevator doors closed. *We've just got to think of some way to change their minds. And it looks like we'd better do it soon!*

"Can I help you?" Mrs. Jefferson asked Caroline, stamping the due date onto a card in a library book and closing it firmly.

Caroline took a deep breath, looking around her to make sure there was no one she knew in the public library. "I wanted to return these," she said shyly, sliding three old, leatherbound books across the counter. "And I was wonder-

47

ing if that book I asked you about last week had been returned."

Mrs. Jefferson took the books from Caroline and examined them closely. "Oh, I remember now." She laughed. "You're the one who's been taking out all of Robert Browning's books."

Caroline lowered her head in embarrassment and twisted nervously at a strand of hair. She wished the librarian would keep her voice down.

"It's funny," Mrs. Jefferson went on. "Up until about a month ago, no one's looked at Browning for years! Other than his poetry, of course," she added quickly. "And then you came along, and he got the business he deserved!"

"I think his poetry is beautiful," Caroline admitted. "He's one of the most romantic people I've ever read."

"Really?" Mrs. Jefferson's eyebrows shot up. "Well, maybe that explains it," she smiled. " 'In the spring a young man's fancy lightly turns to thoughts of love.' Maybe now that the season's right, everyone wants to read Browning."

"Why?" Caroline asked. "Is someone else reading Browning?"

"I should say so!" Mrs. Jefferson laughed. "Someone's reading even more Browning than you are! She's been in here almost every day for the last two weeks. And I think these were the books she was looking for," she added, taking the books Caroline had returned and stacking them neatly on the shelf. "Now, what was her name again?" she wondered aloud. "Lisa? Lucy? I'm sorry, dear, I just can't seem to remember."

"That's OK, Mrs. Jefferson," Caroline said. She had just seen Annie Whitman come into the library, and she wanted to take another book out as quickly as possible. "It doesn't matter."

"I just thought you could form a kind of club," Mrs. Jefferson said vaguely, looking disappointed. "You know, a Browning appreciation club or something."

"Did that book I was waiting for come back?" Caroline asked again, looking nervously at Annie across the crowded reading room.

"Yes, dear!" Mrs. Jefferson exclaimed, taking a dark blue book out from under the counter. "Here it is. Now, you enjoy it," she said happily. Caroline clasped the book in delight, thanked the librarian, and hurried away from the counter.

Outside Caroline dropped the book into her bicycle basket, pulled her bicycle from the rack, and swung her leg over the bar. Her mind was racing as she pedaled home through the beautiful, shady streets. *I wonder what it must have been like to be Elizabeth Barrett Browning*, she thought, barely aware of the sunlight and shade passing over her. *It must have been so wonderful to get letters from Robert Browning—to get them for real, from a real poet.*

Turning into her driveway, Caroline walked her bicycle into the garage, pulling the door closed behind her. Anita was due home in about forty-five minutes, and Caroline had a lot to do before then.

Upstairs, she closed her bedroom door firmly behind her before she opened her portable typewriter on her desk. From her third desk drawer, way at the back, she took out a box of light-blue stationery. Taking a deep breath, Caroline sat down at the desk and slipped a sheet of paper into the typewriter. "My dearest Caroline," she typed. Then she reached for the library book and opened it to the frontispiece.

*Robert Browning: Letters, Volume III,* the book was titled. It contained dozens of Browning's letters. Caroline had gotten so adept at this that she found a good one almost right away. She always had to change a few things to make it perfect, and she never copied a whole letter from Browning, either. That would have been cheating. She always tried to imagine what Adam would really have written to her about, and put in as many details as she could: how the baseball team was doing, what he was writing his history term paper on, and above all—over and over again—how much he missed Caroline, and how he was counting the hours until he would see her again.

The first time Caroline had typed a letter to herself from the imaginary Adam, she'd felt silly. But the letter had been such a big success when she'd read it to friends at school that she felt better about the next one.

Now Caroline couldn't help feeling uneasy about the whole thing. She was getting tired of sneaking around, and it made her feel incredibly sad to type a letter to herself.

But she seemed to be getting deeper and deeper into the story she'd invented. *And besides,* Caroline thought stubbornly, *people will think I'm worthless without Adam. Anita doesn't know about him, and she's pretty good proof of that!*

Caroline still hadn't gotten a chance to tell her sister about Adam. But despite her misgivings about the whole story, Caroline was ready to let Anita know that *somebody* out there thought she was special.

*She may not think more of me for it,* Caroline thought, taking the finished letter carefully out of the typewriter. *But she sure can't think less of me than she does right now.*

# Five

Caroline was listening eagerly for the sound of Anita's car in the driveway. *I've got to get this right*, she told herself. It was one thing to show letters that Adam had supposedly sent her, but faking a telephone call was a much bigger challenge. The barking of the Pearces' toy poodle signaled that Anita was home.

Waiting until she could hear Anita's footsteps in the front hall, Caroline picked up the telephone in the living room and held the receiver to her ear. "Oh, *yes*, Adam," she said after a minute. "Yes, I think so, too. I was so happy to get your letter today," she added loudly, watching her sister hang up her jacket in the front-hall closet. "Oh, wait a minute," she added

quickly. "I think my sister's just come home."
Putting her hand over the receiver, she called
out a greeting to Anita and then resumed her
one-sided conversation.

Under ordinary circumstances Anita would
have gone right through the living room into
the kitchen without even noticing her sister.
But when she heard Caroline talking to a boy,
she slowed down and actually gave her sister a
smile. She went into the kitchen, but Caroline
could tell she was still listening.

It was exactly what Caroline had hoped for.
Now that it was actually happening, she was
ecstatic. It was definitely worth it—all the lying,
the deception. She didn't care that Adam didn't
even exist. The only thing that mattered was
that Anita was paying attention to her. And
she'd even given her little sister an encouraging
smile!

Staying on the phone was harder than she'd
expected, and after another minute or two Caroline made an excuse to hang up. Afraid she
sounded too abrupt, she added hastily, "But I'll
write back to you tonight." After a pause she
added, "Yes, I love you, too. Goodbye, Adam."

Sauntering into the kitchen, Caroline took a
glass from the cupboard and poured herself
some milk. She picked up Anita's copy of *Vogue*
from the counter and sat down at the table, idly

leafing through the pages. In truth, she couldn't have cared less about the fashions. What she was interested in was Anita's reaction to her call—and she didn't have long to wait.

Anita, who'd just finished a cup of yogurt, closed the magazine on Caroline's hand. "Who's Adam?" she asked curiously.

With a little smile on her face, Caroline told her, "Just the most wonderful person on earth."

Anita was clearly skeptical. "Where did you dig up this perfect creature?"

Caroline couldn't use the story she had told the girls at school, about meeting Adam at a party her parents had given. But she had anticipated Anita's question, and she was prepared. "Remember when I went up to Cold Springs with the debating team? I met him there. He was on the other team. We debated each other. He won, and he was so eloquent in his argument that I just had to go up to him afterward and tell him so. Strange as it may seem to you, he was impressed with me, too. Then one thing led to another, and the next thing I knew we were promising to write to each other." She looked at her sister's incredulous expression. "Oh, Anita, he writes the most beautiful letters."

Anita looked curiously at her younger sister. "If they're so great, how come this is the first I've heard of him?"

Caroline lowered her head. "I was afraid to tell you. At first I figured he'd write one, and that would be the end of it, but just the opposite has happened. Through our letters we've fallen in love."

"Does Mom know about him?"

Caroline shook her head. "No, she'd think I'm crazy—like you do."

"Oh, I don't think you're crazy, Caroline. Would you mind showing me these letters? I'd like to see them for myself."

Caroline smiled and stood up. "I'd love to. They're in my room."

Caroline practically skipped up the steps to her bedroom. Jumping on her bed, she carefully lifted up her green-plaid bedspread. Underneath her pillow was a carefully wrapped packet of letters. "Start with the bottom one. That's the first one he sent. That's all of them except for the one I got today."

Anita began to read. " 'My dearest, inexpressibly dearest, Caroline. Your flower is the one flower I have seen, or see or shall see. When it fades I will bless it till it shines again. Caroline, if you meant to make me most exquisitely happy . . . and you did surely mean it . . . well, you've succeeded.' Boy, this Adam's got the poet in him, that's for sure. By the way, what does he look like?"

"He's about six feet two, and he's got dark brown hair and the deepest, brownest eyes I've ever seen. They look like melted chocolate. They're so deep it's like I could see inside his soul just staring at them. He plays baseball, too. I haven't seen him play, naturally, but I know he's got to be good. He's got that athlete's natural grace."

Anita continued to read. " 'Oh, it was a good inspiration that led you through the half-opened auditorium door, and better still, that made me see you standing at the podium.' Boy, he really seems to care about you."

"There's nothing seem-y about it," Caroline corrected. "Face it, Anita, he's the real thing."

Her sister pored over the rest of the letters. After she put down the last one, she said, "I'm really happy for you, Caroline. He sounds like a wonderful guy. He must think you're pretty special, or he'd never write letters like that to you."

Impulsively Caroline hugged her sister. "Thanks for being happy for me. It means a lot to me."

"So when are you going to see him again?" Anita asked.

"I don't know," Caroline admitted. "The distance is a problem. But I hope he can manage to come down here soon."

"Hmm." Anita began to run her fingers

through Caroline's straight red hair. "How would you like me to treat you to a big-sister make-over one of these days?" Anita asked her, looking critically at her sister's haircut.

Caroline's eyes lit up. "Are you serious?" she asked. "Oh, Anita, I'd love it!"

Anita burst out laughing. "We probably shouldn't change too much," she said thoughtfully, "or Adam will never recognize you. Besides, he fell in love with you the way you are."

"I don't care," Caroline said stubbornly. "I bet he'd love me even more when you were through with me," she added hastily.

Anita smiled. "Well, I don't have much time this afternoon," she said thoughtfully. "But if you'll meet me tomorrow afternoon at the mall, we could go shopping together. And I know a great new place that might be able to do something terrific with your hair."

Caroline had to fight to keep the emotion from showing as she gave her sister a hug. It had worked! Anita was finally paying attention to her!

*She's only interested in me right now because of Adam*, a stubborn voice inside reminded her after Anita had left the room. *And Adam is just someone I made up.*

*I don't care*, she thought stubbornly, blinking

back the tears. *It's worth it to finally have Anita's approval. And if it only lasts for a little while—well, it's still better than nothing.*

But as far as Caroline was concerned, things could go on this way for a long, long time. As long as she kept her library books a secret, no one would ever find out about Adam.

And things could stay exactly the way they were.

"This is what's known as teamwork," Elizabeth said with a giggle, opening the door to the Sweet Valley Chamber of Commerce and grinning at her twin.

"I don't know," Jessica said skeptically. "You really think it'll work?"

"I'm not sure," Elizabeth said. "But it is sure worth a try."

The walls of the reception area were covered with posters advertising the upcoming Sweet Valley Centennial Celebration. "Hey, I forgot all about that," Jessica said, pointing to the posters. "That'll help, too."

Elizabeth nodded, smiling at the middle-aged woman who was seated at the receptionist's desk. "May I help you?" the woman asked kindly, taking off her glasses.

Jessica stepped up to the desk, her expression turning very serious. "Yes, ma'am," she said politely, "I think you can. My parents are doing a civic community project, and they asked us to drop by and put them on every mailing list you've got. Anything you can send them would be a big help—brochures on Sweet Valley, pamphlets, news of upcoming events, tourist attractions—everything."

"I'd be delighted to help them," the woman said. "Can you give me their names and address?"

While Elizabeth was looking at the bulletin board, Jessica wrote down her parents' work addresses, as well as their address at home. "That ought to do it," Jessica muttered to her twin. "Can they expect to receive a lot of material?" she asked the woman.

The receptionist laughed. "Well, it depends on how much they can stand. If you really want them to get *all* the material, we could send them dozens of pamphlets."

"I think they'll need it," Jessica said soberly. "Don't you think so, Liz?"

"Oh, yes," Elizabeth said seriously, trying to keep a straight face.

"Now, I don't suppose I can interest either of you two in participating in the centennial celebration, can I?" the woman asked hopefully.

"What sort of things will be going on?" Elizabeth asked.

The receptionist looked excited. "There's going to be a huge parade," she confided. "And an open-air market for all the local merchants; talent contests; beauty contests; fireworks. You name it."

"We could enter the beauty contest," Jessica said after a moment's reflection. "What do you think, Liz?"

"I think we'd better give it some thought," Elizabeth said quickly, shooting Jessica a dirty look. "Thanks so much for all your help," she added, putting a few brochures into her handbag for good measure.

"Do you really think just reminding Mom and Dad of all the good times they've had in Sweet Valley is going to do it?" Jessica asked, following her sister down the steps leading to the parking lot.

"It can't hurt," Elizabeth pointed out. "Why?" she added. "Have you got a better idea?"

Jessica shrugged, tossing her blond hair off one shoulder. "I think you're right, Liz. And it's worth a try. But, remember, there are two sides to every coin." There was a twinkle in her blue-green eyes.

"What do you mean?" Elizabeth asked as they arrived at the bus stop.

"Well, we can start out by making Mom and Dad realize how wonderful Sweet Valley is. But at the same time we can start dropping subtle slurs about San Francisco. The worse we make it look, the better our chances of staying put!"

"Jessica Wakefield," Elizabeth said firmly, "I knew this case wasn't over yet!"

Jessica giggled. "For the first time in days, I'm beginning to think we may just have a chance."

# Six

Caroline looked nervously around the cafeteria, trying to find someone she knew before joining the lunch line. Despite Anita's encouragement, she still felt uneasy about the new outfit she was wearing. For as long as she could remember, Caroline had always dressed conservatively. She liked simple, cotton, button-down shirts, and she felt uncomfortable if they weren't buttoned all the way up to the top. The T-shirt Anita had helped her pick out at the mall had looked harmless enough hanging on the rack. But now that she was wearing it, Caroline felt uncomfortable. It wasn't exactly low-cut, but it *did* have a scooped neckline.

"It makes your new haircut look so much

better," Anita had told her, and that morning Caroline had been tempted to agree with her. But once she'd gotten to school she'd felt self-conscious.

"Hi, Bill," she said cheerfully, falling into line behind Bill Chase. *Maybe it won't be so hard*, she told herself. *If I could only feel more confident about myself, making small talk would be so much easier!* "How's your play coming?" she asked him, taking a tuna-salad plate from the top of the counter.

"OK," Bill said, looking around for his girlfriend DeeDee Gordon before moving up to the cashier. "How'd you know I was writing a play?" he asked, looking closely at Caroline.

Caroline shrugged. "I don't know," she said absently. "I guess someone told me."

"Well, it's coming along pretty well," Bill told her.

"What's it about?" Caroline asked.

"The life of Edwin Booth," Bill said. "He was one of the greatest actors who ever lived."

"Is that why you were talking to Mr. Jaworski this morning?" Caroline asked, her curiosity aroused. Mr. Jaworski was the drama coach at Sweet Valley High.

"Of course not," Bill said quickly. "I was asking him about something else."

"About what?" Caroline asked. She really

didn't mean to pry, but once she'd gotten started she didn't seem to be able to stop herself.

Bill picked up his tray with a frown. "It's none of your business," he said angrily. "What I was talking to Mr. Jaworski about has nothing to do with the competition."

Caroline turned bright red. She hadn't meant to get Bill angry, but somehow she'd put her foot in her mouth again!

"And if you know what's good for you, you'll keep quiet about it," Bill told her, rushing off to join DeeDee on the patio outside.

Caroline sighed. She hadn't handled that very well, she thought uncomfortably. Still, it seemed to her that Bill had been unusually defensive. Perhaps he thought she was still as big a gossip as she used to be. Caroline took her tray into the crowded lunchroom. Or else he really was asking Mr. Jaworski for help on his play. And from the way he was acting, that seemed more likely!

"Caroline," Annie Whitman said angrily, jumping up from her table and coming over to where the redhead was standing. "Would you mind telling me what you think you're trying to do to Ricky and me?"

"What do you mean?" Caroline asked, puzzled.

"That story you've been spreading about Ricky

and Maria is all over school. And I'd appreciate it if you'd just mind your own business. Ricky and Maria are friends, and I couldn't care less about how much they talk to each other! The way you make it sound, I come across like a jealous shrew. Ricky and I almost broke up because of you!"

"I didn't mean to make trouble, Annie," Caroline said sincerely. "I was only—"

"You were only sticking your nose into other people's business, as usual," Annie said bitterly. "Just do me a favor, Caroline, and leave Ricky and me alone." With that, Annie stormed away.

*Boy, is she ever sensitive,* Caroline thought, looking around her unhappily for a place to sit down. *How was I supposed to know she didn't care about Maria?*

Her green eyes lit up as she caught sight of Elizabeth and Todd at a table in the corner. Maybe she could make it up to Liz for embarrassing her at the Dairi Burger, Caroline thought happily, hurrying over to join the couple. If Bill Chase really was cheating on his play, Elizabeth deserved to know about it. It was the least she could do, Caroline told herself, balancing her tray as she came up to the corner table.

"My parents still haven't made up their minds," Elizabeth said wearily for about the tenth time that day, when she saw the redhead approach her.

"I'm not interested in that," Caroline said, putting down her tray. Both Bill's and Annie's warnings were forgotten as she whispered in her best conspiratorial voice, "You were right about Bill Chase. He's definitely going to be real competition for you."

"I already know that," Elizabeth said firmly, turning back to face Todd.

Caroline grabbed her hand to get her attention again. "But did you know he's been getting a lot of help from Mr. Jaworski?"

"But that's against the rules!" Elizabeth cried.

Caroline gasped. "No wonder he got so defensive when I told him I saw him talking with Mr. Jaworski!"

"He did? What did they say?" Elizabeth didn't like the idea of pumping Caroline for information, but if Bill was cheating, she wanted to know about it.

"I wasn't close enough to hear them, but I did see Mr. Jaworski hand Bill a couple of books on acting. And Bill's play is about an actor, you know."

"Hmm." Elizabeth needed time to think about the situation. "Thanks for telling me, Caroline."

"My pleasure, Liz. I've got to run, or else I'd stay and eat with you."

Elizabeth sighed and stared outside at the patio, where Bill Chase was eating his lunch with DeeDee. It was hard for her to imagine an easygoing guy like Bill cheating. Also, Mr. Jaworski was in charge of the contest. He certainly wasn't going to help one of the contestants.

Elizabeth turned to Todd. "What do you think, Todd?"

"I think Caroline's a troublemaker. Mr. Jaworski's not going to give special help to anyone, and I don't think Bill Chase would cheat. I hope Caroline doesn't tell that story to any—"

Elizabeth held up her hand, signaling for Todd to be quiet. Her eyes had wandered over to the table next to Bill's. "Look at that, Todd," she said, pointing to Regina Morrow. "Something's definitely going on over there, and I don't think I like it."

Elizabeth had just seen Bruce Patman approach Regina, who'd been quietly working on her homework. "Is this seat taken?" he asked her.

"Hi, Bruce. Sit down," Regina said, smiling up at him.

Regina Morrow was too new at Sweet Valley High to know that much about Bruce Patman's reputation. She did know Bruce was rich—*everyone* knew that—and that he drove a black Porsche. And from a few of the jokes she'd heard about him, she assumed driving wasn't the only thing Bruce was fast at. But he looked perfectly friendly, and Regina was too open-minded to judge him on the basis of rumors.

"I saw your picture on the cover of that magazine," Bruce said, clearing his throat. "I just wanted to tell you I really liked the article they wrote about you. You must be a pretty special girl, Regina."

Regina laughed, wrinkling her nose. "Not special enough to be able to figure out this math homework." She giggled.

"Let me take a look," Bruce said helpfully, looking at the problem Regina had been struggling with. Within minutes he had shown her a shortcut, and the problem was done.

"Thanks, Bruce," Regina said warmly. He wasn't such a bad guy at all, she thought to herself, sneaking an appreciative look at Bruce's powerful build and chiseled features. She'd really like to get to know him better.

"Hey," Bruce said suddenly, leaning back in his chair. "That article said you like fast cars. Have you ever driven in a Porsche?"

Regina smiled. Bruce looked so nervous she felt flattered. "No, I haven't," she told him. "Why do you ask?" Regina was enjoying Bruce's embarrassment too much to let him off lightly.

"Well, I have one," he told her, clearing his

throat again. "I don't suppose you'd like to go for a ride in it sometime?"

"As a passenger or a driver?" Regina teased him.

Bruce blushed. "Whichever you prefer," he said awkwardly. Bruce had never met a girl who was so obviously unflustered by his advances, and he didn't know quite what to say.

"You're on," Regina said, smiling. "How about this afternoon?"

"OK," Bruce said, looking relieved. He stood up. "I don't have tennis practice today, so this afternoon is just fine. Where should I meet you?"

"Oh, I'll find you," Regina said. As Bruce started to walk away, Regina called after him, "And thanks for helping me with my math." She had no way of knowing how much the conversation had shaken Bruce or how his heart quickened at the thought of seeing her again after school. All she knew was that she was glad she'd given him a chance. And she had a feeling that the afternoon was going to be a lot of fun.

Caroline set her tray down next to Lila and Jessica, giving them both a big smile. "I'm so glad I found you guys," she said happily, pulling up a chair.

"So are we," Jessica mumbled, rolling her eyes at Lila.

But Lila wasn't paying attention. She was staring at Caroline, trying to decide why the redhead looked so much better that day. "Did you get your hair cut, Caroline?" she asked.

Caroline nodded, taking a bite of her sandwich. "I hope Adam likes it," she said, sneaking a look at Jessica's expression. So far that day, she'd completely botched things up, she thought. Maybe mentioning Adam would make things better again.

"I think it looks nice," Lila said, taking a spoonful of yogurt. "Who knows?" she added archly, catching Jessica's eye across the table. "By the time Adam sees it, it may have grown out again."

Caroline bit her lip. She didn't like the way Lila sounded. Was it possible she and Jessica were already getting suspicious? "I don't think so," she said firmly. "He wanted me to visit him this weekend, but he's got a baseball game on Saturday, so I'll probably go next weekend," she explained.

Lila looked unconvinced. "Why doesn't he come here?" she asked. "We're all dying to meet him, Caroline."

"He will," Caroline said lightly. "Look, Lila, Cold Springs is pretty far away. You can't expect him to dash down here all the time, can you? Besides," she added suddenly, a flash of inspiration coming to her, "he really can't afford all that gasoline. He doesn't have much money."

"Oh," Lila said distastefully, putting down her yogurt. The thought of a boyfriend without money seemed to make her lose her appetite. "What a shame."

"It's OK with me," Caroline said cheerfully. "Letters are much more romantic, and he can afford stamps!"

"Did you get another letter from him?" Jessica asked.

Caroline nodded. "Yesterday." She sighed, a dreamy expression coming over her face.

"And I suppose you've got it with you?" Jessica continued, a funny look in her eyes.

"Of course," Caroline assured her. "I carry Adam's letters everywhere I go. That way I can reread them whenever I feel like it."

"Let's see his latest poetic effort," Jessica said.

Caroline passed her the typewritten sheet she'd folded up in her bag.

"Let me see it," Lila cried, snatching it from Jessica's hand. " 'My dearest Caroline,' " she read out loud. " 'Your letter came this morning, and the promise it contained of another made me restless all day . . .' "

"Hey, look at this part," Jessica exclaimed, reading over Lila's shoulder. " 'Now I will go out and walk where I can be alone, and think thoughts of you, and love you. I will look in the direction of Sweet Valley, and send my heart there . . .' "

"Good Lord," Lila interrupted. "Is this guy for real? He sounds like something from 'Masterpiece Theatre.' "

Caroline blushed. "Of course he's for real," she lied. "He's just very romantic."

"OK, when do we get to see this romantic hero in the flesh?" Jessica asked. "I want to see if he looks as good as he sounds."

"You'll meet him," Caroline said evasively. She didn't like the look Jessica gave Lila. How much longer, she wondered, would they be satisfied with letters?

Suddenly, Caroline didn't feel very well. It had just occurred to her that she was swimming in dangerous waters. And with sharks like Jessica and Lila about, she might not make it out alive.

# Seven

Alice Wakefield rushed through the front door at seven o'clock that evening. "Hi, everyone," she called out. She removed her navy blazer and hung it in the closet, then headed toward the kitchen. "Sorry I'm late. Everything ran overtime today. I'll hurry and get dinner ready." She stopped short in the dining room when she noticed that the table had been set with the Wakefields' good china and silver. Something was cooking, and it smelled delicious. "What's this?" she asked.

"Surprise, Mom." Jessica walked over and kissed her mother. She was wearing an apron over her shorts and T-shirt. "Liz and I were feeling rotten about the way we've been acting. We hope this dinner'll make up for it."

"Oh, you didn't have to go to all this trouble," her mother said, laughing. "A simple apology would have been enough. Where's Liz?"

"Right here, Mom." Elizabeth walked in from the kitchen with a vase full of flowers.

"Amaryllis! How lovely," she exclaimed. "Where did you find them?"

"At Petal Pushers. They always have the best flowers," Elizabeth said. "Jessica and I wanted to do more than just apologize. We've been acting like a couple of brats lately. Will you forgive us?"

"I could never stay mad at you girls," Mrs. Wakefield said, taking a seat at the table. "Something smells wonderful. What's for dinner?"

"You'll see," Jessica said mysteriously. "But you'll have to wait till Dad gets home."

"Did someone mention me?" As if on cue Ned Wakefield came into the dining room.

"Sure, sit down, Dad," Elizabeth said. "I hope you're hungry, 'cause we've got something special planned for tonight."

He looked at the table. "Flowers? China? Hmm, I smell a bribe here."

"Not at all," Elizabeth said, bringing the salad to the table. Everybody sat down and began to eat. "Jessica and I are ready to accept your decision on the move. Whatever you want to do—we'll go along with it willingly."

"Liz is right, Mom," Jessica said sweetly.

Looking warily at her husband, Mrs. Wakefield put down her fork. "I'm glad to hear that. My compliments to whomever made the salad. The dressing is superb."

"Thanks, Mom," Jessica said. "We got it at Season's Gourmet Shop. It's made with that special Dijon mustard you like so much."

"And just wait till the next course," Elizabeth added. "It's an old favorite of yours, veal parmesan, from Vito's."

Mrs. Wakefield's face lit up. "I can't remember the last time I had one of his meals. Funny, though, there was a time we used to take out meals from Vito's almost once a week."

"I know, Mom." Elizabeth grinned and gave Jessica a wink.

"Well, girls, Vito still makes a great veal," Mrs. Wakefield said when the meal was over. "It was much better than what I had in mind for tonight."

"You deserved a night off from cooking," Jessica said.

"But we're not done yet," Elizabeth said, rising. She went to the refrigerator and pulled out a white bakery box.

"Don't tell me," Mrs. Wakefield said. "Lemon chiffon pie from Caster's?"

"Oh, Mom, you spoiled the surprise," Elizabeth said, pretending to be more disappointed than she was. "But you're right."

Mrs. Wakefield put her napkin to her lips. "I feel as if it's my birthday. Everything's been wonderful, girls."

"Thanks, Mom, but I have to admit I have an ulterior motive," Elizabeth said.

Mrs. Wakefield nodded knowingly. "I thought so."

"I thought you weren't going to tell her," Jessica hissed.

"I have to now," Elizabeth admitted. "See, I wanted to make sure you were in a good mood. I'm going to read my play to you tonight. I still have to rework some parts, but I need to hear how it sounds."

"Great. You fill us up, then make us sick to our stomachs." Jessica groaned.

"That wasn't called for, Jessica," her father warned.

"I'm a little nervous," Elizabeth continued, undaunted. "It's the first time I've read this play out loud to anyone. But I've got to do it now. The competition's coming up." She got up to get her play, and as she left the room she remarked casually, "By the way, did you know this was the only contest like this in the state? We're so lucky to go to Sweet Valley High. Don't you think so, Jess?"

Jessica laughed. "You're not kidding," she said, ignoring the smile her parents exchanged.

Once everyone was gathered in the den, Elizabeth began to read her one-act play. Jessica was only half-listening to her sister, wondering how she was going to get out of doing the dishes that were still in the sink, when something Elizabeth said made her sit up and take notice. "Sorry, Liz," Jessica interrupted. "I didn't quite hear that last part. Would you mind repeating it?"

"Sure," Elizabeth said good-naturedly. "As I was saying, Elizabeth Barrett was in her study, reading the letter sent to her by her beloved Robert. " 'My Ba, your letter came as it ought last night, and the promise it contained of another made me restless all the morning, to no purpose . . .' "

As Elizabeth was reading, a sense of déjà vu fell over Jessica. She'd heard those words before—she was sure of it—but as far as she could remember, she'd never read any of Robert Browning's letters. Where had she heard them then?

" '. . . I will go out and walk where I can be alone, and think out all my thoughts of you, and bless you, and love you with nothing to intercept the blessing and the love. I will look in the direction of London—' "

"That's it!" Jessica exclaimed, quickly covering her mouth when she realized she'd spoken out loud. Elizabeth had stopped reading. "Oh, go on, Liz," Jessica said with a wave of her hand. "I was just so moved by that last part I couldn't help myself. He was so romantic."

"Yes, he was," Elizabeth said, not really convinced that her twin's outburst was a sentimental one. She looked back down at her papers. " '. . . and send my heart there. Dear, dear love, I kiss you . . .' "

Jessica clasped her arms around her legs and listened with new concentration. Yes, she concluded, some of the words were changed, updated, but there was no doubt about it—these were Adam's letters!

If there was an Adam. Jessica's mind began to churn with the possibilities. *Oh, Liz, hurry up*, she said to herself. *I don't know how long I can keep this to myself!*

Fortunately Jessica didn't have long to wait. Elizabeth completed reading her play a few minutes later. Her twin was the first to rise and give her a standing ovation. As her parents followed suit, Jessica said, "Bravo, Liz. It's the best play I ever heard. Sorry I can't stay and help you celebrate. I've got an important call to make."

She ran to her room, slammed the door shut behind her, and dialed Lila's number. "Lila, we've been made fools of," she declared, the instant Lila picked up the phone.

"Jessica? What on earth are you talking about?"

"Caroline Pearce. Those letters she's been passing off as her boyfriend's are fakes! They weren't written by a sixteen-year-old boy. They were written by a dead poet!"

"Are you sure?"

"I heard them with my own ears. Liz put them in her play about Elizabeth Barrett Browning. They're the same letters Robert Browning wrote to her over a hundred years ago!"

"I still don't see what you're getting so worked up about," Lila said, dismissing her friend's agitation. "So Adam's not a poet, he's a plagiarizer. I'll bet Caroline doesn't even know."

"Or maybe she knows all too well. I've always thought there was something strange about this Adam guy. I mean, how realistic is it for some fabulous, romantic guy to fall head over heels in love with Caroline Pearce? When you come right down to it, it's practically science fiction!"

"What are you trying to say, Jess?"

"I think Caroline wrote those letters herself.

It makes a lot of sense. They're always type-written, for one thing. And wouldn't a guy who's supposedly as romantic as Adam write words like that out by hand? It's so much more personal than typing. And she's gotten so many of them! If Adam's as busy as she says he is, when does he have the time to write them all?"

"You already said he didn't make them up from scratch. And as far as the typing goes, the guy probably has sloppy handwriting. Caroline never said he was perfect."

"Well, I'm not going to believe he really exists until I see him with my own eyes. When did Caroline say he was coming down for a visit?"

"She didn't," Lila admitted. "She says it's hard for him to make the trip."

"Sure it's hard. It's impossible for a ghost to come to life."

"You don't believe he's real," Lila remarked.

"And I won't believe it until I see him with my own eyes."

"They can't keep up a letter-writing romance forever," Lila reasoned. "They're going to have to see each other sometime. Maybe we can work on her, Jessica. We can force her to introduce him to us. I'd like to see him, anyway."

"I'm all for that," Jessica said. "But I'll bet you anything that she tries to get out of it somehow. Let's not waste any time. Maybe we can get something out of her at the sorority meeting tomorrow."

"If she shows up, you mean."

"Caroline? Are you kidding? She's the only one of us with a perfect attendance record. She'll be there."

After Jessica had hung up the phone, she sat perfectly still for a minute, an oddly satisfied expression on her pretty face. She'd heard just about enough from Caroline about Adam, and Jessica couldn't wait to confront her.

Ordinarily Jessica might have shrugged the whole thing off, figuring she had more important things to worry about than where Caroline's boyfriend—real or invented—got his love letters from. But Jessica associated Caroline with the possibility of a move to San Francisco. Caroline might not have had anything to do with Mrs. Wakefield's decision, but she *had* been the one to break the bad news. And Jessica couldn't forgive her for that. *No, that girl has meddled once too often*, Jessica told herself. *And I'm going to make sure she's good and sorry—if it's the last thing I do in Sweet Valley!*

# Eight

The Pi Beta Alpha meeting was held in Casey's Place the next afternoon. All of the sorority sisters were present, except Elizabeth Wakefield and Enid Rollins, who thought the sorority was more of an excuse to socialize than anything else, and who were members in name only. After the meeting, everyone sat around eating and talking. Caroline had ordered a chocolate milk shake, but she wasn't paying much attention to it. She was reading Adam's latest letter to the group of girls who had gathered around her booth. Her face was flushed with pleasure. No one had ever cared about her at a sorority meeting before, but that day she was the center of attention!

"Sorry to interrupt," Lila Fowler said suddenly, breaking through the attentive audience, "but Jessica and I need to talk to Caroline for a second."

*Uh-oh*, Caroline thought unhappily. *Here comes trouble.* Her audience dispersed, and Lila slid next to her in the booth while Jessica sat on the other side.

"I was just reading Adam's letter again," Caroline said uneasily, looking from Jessica to Lila and back to Jessica again.

"Isn't that a coincidence!" Lila exclaimed. "We were just talking about him. We were wondering when he's coming to visit."

"I'm not sure," Caroline said nervously. "Soon, though."

"How soon?" Jessica asked. "Sometime in the next year?"

"Of course," Caroline answered, biting her lip.

"In the next six months?" Lila asked.

"Sure."

"How about in the next month?" said Jessica.

Caroline finally saw where the conversation was leading to. "Uh—I don't know."

"You've got to see him sometime," Jessica pressed on. "Unless—maybe you have no intention of seeing him at all."

"Of course I do. I'm going up to visit him this weekend," she blurted out.

"Good," said Lila, pleased with Caroline's response. "That leaves the next weekend free for him to come here. We're going to throw a party for him."

Caroline gasped. "You don't have to do that, Lila."

"It would be our pleasure," Lila said. "Sort of our way of saying welcome to Sweet Valley."

Caroline hesitated. "Adam's kind of shy. I don't think he'd like the idea of a party."

"Come on," Jessica said. "He hardly comes across as shy in those letters."

"But you don't really know him," Caroline insisted.

"Don't I?" Jessica pressed. "You've read me all his letters. I feel like I know him pretty well. And I'm sure he'd *love* a party in his honor."

"Gee, Jess, I really don't know," Caroline mumbled.

"What's wrong, Caroline?" Lila asked, pretending to be surprised. "I can't believe you'd want to turn down the opportunity to star at your own party. It's the chance of a lifetime."

"I know," Caroline said miserably.

"So what's the problem?" Lila pressed.

"Well—"

84

"There is none. It's all set," Jessica finished for her.

Lila added, "We'll have it at my house. We'll invite everyone. It'll be great."

"Sure. It'll be fun," Caroline said weakly.

"So how's next weekend? Will Adam be able to make it then?" Lila asked.

Caroline shrugged. If only they'd let her alone!

"Ask him in your next letter. I guarantee he'll say yes," Jessica said.

Caroline watched as Jessica and Lila got up and sauntered over to the counter to order ice-cream sundaes. Her own milk shake was still sitting in front of her, virtually untouched. The last thing Caroline could think about was eating. In fact, now that it occurred to her, she felt queasy.

She barely knew what to worry about first. Had Lila and Jessica somehow caught on to the fact that Adam's letters weren't genuine? Why else would they be so eager to get Adam down here?

And even worse, how was she going to satisfy them? *I've really made a mess of things*, Caroline said to herself unhappily. And as far as she could tell, there was no way out of the mess she'd created.

*       *       *

"I don't understand this," Mrs. Wakefield said, sorting through the mail, a puzzled expression on her face. "Ned, are you still getting brochures from the Chamber of Commerce?"

Mr. Wakefield laughed. "Mrs. Kelly told me I've gotten about two dozen this week," he told her.

"Brochures?" Jessica asked innocently. "What sort of brochures?"

Mr. and Mrs. Wakefield exchanged glances. "Information about Sweet Valley," Mrs. Wakefield said lightly. "I've been getting a pile of them at the office, and we're getting them here, too."

"Hmm," Mr. Wakefield said, picking up one of the glossy pamphlets. "Las Palmas Canyon. I haven't been out there in years. We ought to take a drive out there this weekend, Alice."

"Oh, you probably won't have time," Jessica said innocently, opening the newspaper and cutting out an article with a pair of scissors.

"Jess, I haven't even looked at that yet!" her father complained. "What are you doing?"

"I've got to do a project for my history class," Jessica told him. "We're each supposed to cover a topic in current events."

"What's your topic?" her father asked, picking up one of the articles. "Four Killed in San Francisco Quake," the headline ran. A smile broke over Mr. Wakefield's face as he picked up the other articles. "Blaze Destroys Frisco Hotel," one claimed. "Crime in San Francisco—Can It Be Stopped?" another wondered. "Drugs in the City," the last was titled.

"I can't help it, Daddy," Jessica said solemnly, arranging the articles in a neat pile. "I'm supposed to cover natural and unnatural disasters. Can I help it if so many happen to take place in San Francisco?"

"Unnatural disasters?" Elizabeth said, coming into the living room. "What are you talking about, Jess—your bedroom?"

Jessica gave her twin an injured look and shook her head. "It's a sad fact, Daddy," she continued. "Ken Matthews is covering urban blight. It's amazing how tough life is in big cities."

"Like San Francisco, I suppose?" her mother asked, smiling.

Jessica shrugged. "There are lots of advantages, too," she pointed out. "Who cares about little things like smog or drugs or crime when you've got all those theaters and restaurants?"

"Speaking of restaurants," Elizabeth piped up, "Jessica and I have a surprise for you. We want to treat you to a night out on the town. When was the last time you two had dinner at Tiberino's?" she asked, her blue-green eyes twinkling.

Mr. Wakefield winked at his wife behind the twins' back. "Tiberino's?" he asked solemnly. "Why, I'd say it's been a long time. How long *has* it been, Alice?"

Tiberino's was Mr. and Mrs. Wakefield's favorite restaurant. Ned Wakefield had proposed to Alice there, and they had often gone there on their anniversaries. It was still run by Sal Ciardi, a round-faced Italian who'd known the Wakefields all their lives. Mr. Wakefield used to claim you couldn't find better lasagna than Tiberino's this side of Rome.

"A long time," Mrs. Wakefield agreed, smiling at her husband. "It would be nice to have a meal there," she added.

"Good," Elizabeth said. "Then it's settled. Just let us know what night is best for you, and we'll make reservations. After all," she pointed out, "if we're really going to move, you'll probably never get to eat at Tiberino's again."

"Still," Jessica said quickly, "there will be lots of restaurants in San Francisco. There's always Chinatown," she pointed out.

Elizabeth had to fight to contain a giggle. Her father was allergic to Chinese food, and Jessica knew it as well as she did.

"Not bad," Jessica whispered to her twin when their parents had left the room. "But I think it's time to step up the action a little."

"What do you mean?" Elizabeth asked.

Jessica looked furtively out the living room door, making sure her parents were out of earshot. "I mean," she whispered, "that I've got to think of some way to get Dad out to Las Palmas Canyon this weekend."

Elizabeth shook her head admiringly. "It's a good thing you're on my side, Jess. I'd hate to ever have you scheming against me!"

"Who, me? Scheming?" Jessica asked, her turquoise eyes wide with innocence.

Elizabeth shook her head. "You heard me," she said firmly. It was hard to imagine anything worse than being subjected to one of Jessica's schemes. Only right then, Elizabeth thought, even Jessica had too much on her mind to get herself into trouble. *And I'm sure there have got to be one or two people who are glad Jessica's out of commission.*

But Elizabeth had no idea of the plans Jessica had in store for Caroline Pearce.

# Nine

Caroline was at school almost an hour early on Friday morning. She'd barely slept the night before, and she knew she looked terrible. She had big circles under her eyes, and her skin was so pale she looked ill. *I've got two hopes*, she muttered to herself, opening the main door to Sweet Valley High and walking quickly through the deserted hallways. *First, I've got to get as much mileage as I can from this weekend. Everyone's got to believe I really spent the weekend in Cold Springs. And I'd better have hard-core proof that I was there!*

Caroline already had some proof. Her cousin Sally had dated a senior on the Cold Springs football team the previous year, and she'd given

Caroline one of his T-shirts when they'd broken up. Nobody at school knew about Sally, and Caroline could wear the T-shirt to school on Monday and claim it was a present from Adam. But Caroline knew she needed more than a T-shirt to keep Lila and Jessica at bay. And that was why she was at school so early, so she could put her second plan into effect.

Tiptoeing across the hall to the *Oracle* office, Caroline turned the doorknob and was relieved to find the door unlocked. It was a long shot, but a few weeks earlier, she'd overheard Penny Ayala, the editor of the school paper, complaining about all the space the old newspapers from other schools were taking up. *If there's a paper from Cold Springs in here, I can find a picture on the sports page and claim it's Adam,* Caroline thought. Holding her breath, she slipped inside and closed the door behind her.

She flipped on the light switch and looked around the room. The bookcase in the far corner looked promising, and she quickly padded over to it. On the top shelf was a stack of newspapers. Caroline reached up with one hand to remove them, but she didn't quite get a grip on all of them, and about eight or nine issues fell in a half circle in front of her. Cursing silently, she picked them up and took them to a nearby desk.

A look at the top newspaper on the pile showed her she was on the right track. It was from Big Mesa High School. She thumbed her way through the stack until she found what she was looking for: the school newspaper from Cold Springs High. She leafed through it eagerly, searching for the sports section. On the next to last page she found exactly what she needed.

She ripped out part of the page, then put the rest of the paper back on the shelf with the others. Then she folded the clipping and put it in her pocketbook. *Maybe this will hold them for a while*, she thought.

"I got another letter from Adam," Caroline told Lila and Jessica at lunchtime. "He's really excited that I'm coming up for the weekend. I can't wait," she said ecstatically, dropping the newspaper clipping casually on the table.

"What's that?" Lila demanded, pouncing on the clipping.

"Oh, *that*," Caroline said. "It's nothing. You can't even really see him in that picture."

"This is Adam?" Jessica asked, snatching the clipping and looking at it critically. "I thought you said he played baseball," Jessica pointed out. "This is a basketball picture." It was hard to make out anything in the snapshot but a blur of arms reaching for a basket.

"I know," Caroline said confidently. "It's from last season. He just wanted me to have *something*. You can't see him very well, but there he is," she added, pointing to the least blurry pair of arms. "I can't *wait* to see him," she said, hugging herself in anticipation.

Lila and Jessica exchanged glances. "*We* can't wait to see him either," Jessica said firmly. "Be sure to tell him about next weekend. We're counting on his being here for our party."

Caroline gulped. "Well, I'll ask him," she said uncertainly.

"Don't ask him," Lila advised. "*Tell* him. You're new to the dating scene, Caroline, or you'd know that's the way you have to deal with guys!"

*Oh, dear*, Caroline thought in dismay. Plan number two hadn't succeeded very well. She'd just have to make sure that on Monday everyone was convinced she'd had a wonderful time in Cold Springs over the weekend.

Early Saturday afternoon the phone rang in the Wakefields' house. After several rings Mr. Wakefield picked it up.

"Hello, Daddy? It's me, Jessica. I've got a big problem. The car's not working right. It's sputtering and stalling, and now I can't seem to get it started at all. Could you come pick me up?"

"Sure, Jessica," her father answered. "Where are you?"

"I'm out at Las Palmas Canyon. I'm calling you from the country store. The car's parked on the highway about a half mile beyond here."

"What are you doing all the way out there?" Mr. Wakefield asked.

"I'll explain later. Can you come?"

"All right, I'll leave now. Give me half an hour."

Jessica hung up the phone. Whistling softly, she walked out to the parking lot, got in the red Fiat, and drove half a mile down the narrow country road. She parked the car on the grassy shoulder, under the shade of one of the few Douglas firs that dotted the landscape, and began to wait. She knew her father would come to her rescue, even though she did have to stretch the truth about the car breaking down. It was just a minor fib, really. No big deal. Not when there was a more important objective to be achieved.

Like getting her father out there.

Las Palmas Canyon was a steep gorge about twenty miles northeast of Sweet Valley. The two-lane highway that skirted its perimeter twisted and turned through some of the most spectacular scenery in the area. Jessica had parked near the top of the canyon. Below her was a rocky, shrub-covered incline that led to a stream, which cut through the base of the canyon. The buttercups that dotted the landscape gave an added splash of color to the deep carpet of green alfalfa grass. Not too far away, about a mile or so in from the road, was a sparkling waterfall that fed the stream. Ahead of her was a panoramic skyscape of the distant mountains and evergreen-covered hills that lay just beyond the canyon. A hazy film partly obscured the view to the left, but out on the horizon, the deep blue of the Pacific Ocean could be seen.

While she waited for her father, Jessica popped a tape into the Fiat's cassette player and turned up the volume so the music echoed in the otherwise still air. Half an hour later, Ned Wakefield's rust-brown LTD came speeding down the road. He pulled up behind her.

"Let me see what's wrong," he said, approaching her car. He lifted the hood and looked inside. "Nothing wrong here," he said after a quick inspection. "Let's fire her up and see what happens."

He ordered Jessica to turn on the ignition. When the engine came to life, Jessica gasped. "How did that happen? The car practically died on me before."

Mr. Wakefield shrugged. "It may need a new

battery. Let it run for a few minutes. Then I'll follow you home. This way, if you stall out again, I'll be able to give you a jump.''

"OK, Daddy," Jessica said, getting out of her car. She turned to him. "It's beautiful here, isn't it?"

Mr. Wakefield looked around him and smiled. "I'd almost forgotten. It's been so long since I've driven out here. What made you come today?"

"It's so peaceful here, Daddy. I come out here a lot when I've got something on my mind. It's a great place for inspiration, too."

Mr. Wakefield nodded in understanding. "I used to come out here a lot, too, whenever I had a tough case I wanted to think about."

"Why did you stop?"

"I don't know," he said slowly. "I stopped having the time, I guess. It's stupid, though. I should try to get out here more often."

"As long as we're still around here, you mean."

Her father sighed deeply. "Yes."

"I bet there are a lot of places around here you'll miss."

Mr. Wakefield continued to gaze at the country-side. "When you spend your whole life in one place, you store up a lot of memories. I remember when I was a kid I used to go on overnight hikes through these hills."

"I remember the first time you took us out here for a picnic," Jessica said wistfully. "Liz tried to scare me by telling me the bears were going to come and eat me up, but I didn't believe her." She stopped as she saw something move in the canyon. "Hey, look, Dad. Over there. It's a deer!"

"I think there's more than one," her father said, pointing at the outcropping of rock from which the first deer emerged.

"You're right," Jessica said, still keeping the enthusiasm in her voice. Two more deer, one of them a fawn, came into view and pranced across the ledge. "I bet you don't see too many deer in San Francisco."

"No, I'm afraid not," Mr. Wakefield said. Jessica thought he sounded terribly sad. And that was exactly the response she'd wanted. He turned back to his car. "You ready to go now?"

"Sure." Jessica hopped into the Fiat. *Mission accomplished*, she thought as she headed back to Sweet Valley.

About two miles from home Jessica stopped at a red light across from the Farmer's Market. She was about to change the tape in the cassette player when she saw a girl coming out of the store, a heavy bag of groceries in her arms.

Jessica would know that red hair anywhere. Caroline Pearce. *So,* Jessica thought, *she hasn't gone out of town after all.* "Wait till Lila hears about this!" Jessica muttered as she stepped on the gas pedal.

"You saw *who*?" As Jessica suspected, Lila was shocked by Jessica's report. "But Caroline said she was going to Cold Springs this weekend. Are you *sure* you saw her?"

"It was Caroline. I think she saw me, too," Jessica insisted.

"But why would she lie to us?"

"Probably just to keep us happy. She's trying to stall us, Lila, to buy some time to figure out how she's going to produce a guy who doesn't exist. I say we call her bluff."

"OK. We'll pin her down on Monday morning," Lila said. "No one's going to make a fool out of us. So help me, if you're right and she didn't spend the weekend in Cold Springs, Caroline Pearce is in for the roughest week of her life."

# Ten

"So, Caroline, how was your weekend?" Lila asked. She and Jessica were waiting by the redhead's locker on Monday morning, ready to pounce.

*I'm dying to hear how she squirms out of this one,* Jessica thought. She figured Caroline would have no choice now but to confess the truth, that there never really was an Adam.

But Caroline had a surprise for her. "It was the best time ever," she gushed. "We had the most wonderful time together."

"I'll bet," Jessica said sarcastically.

"And look what he gave me!" Caroline zipped open her jacket. Proudly she revealed a white T-shirt with blue lettering. The inscription read:

Property of the Cold Springs Athletic Department.

Jessica's eyes widened in surprise. "Where did you get that?"

"I told you! Adam gave it to me." Caroline smiled dreamily, as if trying to recapture the moment. "It's funny, in a way. He was really apologetic because it wasn't something romantic like roses or jewelry. But he thought I'd like it because it's just like the shirt he wears at baseball practice. I don't really care. I may wear it every day till it disintegrates."

Lila shot Jessica a look as if to say, *What's going on here?* "So tell us what you did."

Caroline finished taking off her jacket and hung it up neatly on the hook inside her locker. "I got there Friday evening. Adam picked me up at the bus station and took me home to meet his mother. She had a special dinner waiting for us. She's so nice. She's an English teacher. I guess that's where Adam gets his writing talent from. Saturday I watched his team play baseball. Adam only scored two runs, but he caught a fly ball that won his team the game. Afterward he took me out to a very fancy restaurant for dinner. We had a table for two and ate by candlelight. It was *so* romantic! Then we went driving for a while. I'm not going to go into the details here, but let me just say I can't think of a better way to spend a Saturday night! Yesterday he took me on a picnic. We hiked in the woods and continued what we started in the car the night before."

"It sounds too good to be true," Lila said, amazed.

"I wished I didn't have to leave," Caroline said.

"Then you must have made plans to see him again soon, right?" Jessica asked. "Did you tell him about the party?"

"Oh, yeah, he said he'd love to come, but the distance is a problem—" Caroline began.

"But an easy problem," Lila broke in. "After all he's only two hours away. That's hardly anything at all, really."

"There's more," Caroline continued. "I told you Adam doesn't have much money. And after all he spent on dinner Saturday night—"

"You call that a problem?" Lila said. "I bet if you were able to scrape together the money for the bus ticket, he'd come, wouldn't he?"

Caroline stared down at her loafers. "I'm short of cash myself, Lila."

"But what if you already had the ticket?" Lila flicked open her wallet and dangled a bus ticket in front of her. "Like this one?"

Caroline backed away. "Lila, I—I couldn't," she stammered. "I could never think of taking anything from you."

"Don't you want to see Adam again?"

"Of course I do," Caroline said.

"Then take it," Lila said, slapping the ticket in Caroline's palm. "I insist. Consider it a present. I hate to see two people in love separated. It's so sad."

Caroline looked at the ticket in her hand. It was only paper, but it felt like a thousand-pound weight to her. "I-I don't know what to say."

Jessica flashed one of her too-sweet smiles. "Just say you're going to invite Adam down this weekend."

"But he might have a game," she pointed out.

Lila shook her head. "I had John check out the schedule. Cold Springs is off till next Tuesday."

"See? There's nothing to keep him from coming," Jessica said, "especially when he finds out about the party."

"That's right, Caroline, it's going to be the biggest thing to hit this town in ages," Lila added. "I plan to see him there, and I won't take no for an answer."

Caroline took a deep breath. What could she say? Obviously she couldn't get out of this one. "We'll be there," she said, sighing. "You can count on it."

But Jessica wasn't through with Caroline yet. "You know," she said innocently, twisting a silky strand of hair around her finger, "you really should read one of Adam's letters to Liz, Caroline. She's an expert on love letters these days."

"What do you mean?" Caroline asked warily.

Jessica gave Lila a sly smile. "Well, you know she's writing her play about Robert Browning and Elizabeth Barrett Browning, and she'll be reading it at the competition on Friday night," she said casually. "Browning was a real ace at love letters. Don't you think so, Lila?"

Lila giggled. "Not as good as Adam," she replied.

Caroline swallowed hard, watching the two girls walk away. She felt miserable. *They know about the letters. They probably know Adam's a complete fake. And when Elizabeth reads her play, the whole school's going to know!*

*So*, Caroline wondered, blinking back tears, *what in the world do I do now?*

Elizabeth stared down at her notebook after putting the finishing touches on her play. She was proud of the work she'd done, but her pride didn't do much to lift her spirits. Her parents still hadn't given Jessica and her a firm answer about San Francisco, and not even Todd could convince her to stay calm. She'd wasted almost half her study hall stitting in the lounge and staring out the windows. She sighed. This wasn't very productive.

"Hi, Liz!" a cheerful voice exclaimed. Elizabeth's brow cleared as she saw Regina Morrow approaching. *At least someone around here's in a good mood*, she thought. She'd never seen Regina look quite so beautiful. Her ivory complexion was blooming, and her blue eyes were sparkling.

"How was your weekend?" Regina asked, sinking into the chair next to Elizabeth.

"OK, I guess. Todd and I are both kind of anxious about my parents' decision. But I'm trying not to worry before I have to."

Regina's brow wrinkled. "You poor thing," she said softly. "Believe me, I can sympathize. I remember how hard it used to be on me when I had to leave a school I'd gotten used to. And I didn't even have a boyfriend then!"

Elizabeth's ears perked up. Boyfriend? Was Regina really serious about Bruce Patman? Elizabeth tried not to show her worry. "You and Bruce have been spending a lot of time together lately, haven't you?" she asked.

Regina nodded. "He's so wonderful, Liz. I've

never had so much fun with a guy before. It turns out we have a lot in common," she went on, her voice lifting with enthusiasm.

*A lot in common?* Elizabeth wondered silently. Regina was one of the nicest people she'd ever met, and Bruce Patman was selfish, snobbish, and mean. What could Regina and Bruce possibly have in common? Elizabeth didn't want to put a damper on Regina's good spirits, but she was really worried about the girl. "Are you sure he's right for you?" she asked quietly. "Isn't he kind of—"

Regina cut her off. "Oh, Liz. I know what everyone says about Bruce. But it's just not true! He's incredibly nice to me, and so considerate!"

*That sounds like Bruce,* Elizabeth thought. *Or at least it sounds like Bruce on the make. Once he gets what he wants from Regina, he'll drop her.*

But Elizabeth didn't want to disillusion Regina. "I'm glad if you're glad," she said, trying to sound happier than she felt.

Regina laughed. "Don't look so worried," she said reproachfully. "Believe me, Liz, Bruce Patman is the best thing to have happened to me in ages!"

Elizabeth watched Regina bounce up from

her chair and walk out of the lounge. *I just hope Regina know's what she's doing. Because when it comes to Bruce Patman, it isn't a case of playing with fire—it's more like playing with a raging inferno!*

# Eleven

"I think our plan is working, Jess," Elizabeth said, leaning across the lunch table. "Dad's definitely softening."

"How can you tell? This morning at breakfast all he and Mom wanted to talk about was the move. And he's having a meeting with a lawyer from San Francisco this afternoon. It sounds pretty dismal to me."

"You weren't listening, Jess. Didn't you hear the *way* he talked about that meeting? He didn't sound too enthusiastic to me. And what kind of law firm would want to hire someone who isn't jumping at the chance to be with them? I think he realizes now that Sweet Valley is where he really belongs."

"So why would he bother going through with this interview?"

"For Mom's sake," Elizabeth explained. "It makes perfect sense, doesn't it? Dad wants to make Mom feel really important, so he goes along with the idea of moving, providing, of course, that he can get a job up there, too. But he really doesn't want to move, so he just goes through the motions of looking for a job. Then, when nothing materializes, he tells Mom she can't accept her job because he can't find a new one. End of story."

Jessica nodded slowly. "In its own confusing way that makes sense, Liz. Except for one thing. Mom said a job offer like hers comes along once in a lifetime. What if she doesn't want to give it up? What if she insists on taking it anyway?"

Elizabeth dismissed the thought. "Mom wouldn't do that."

"Oh, no? You thought she wouldn't even give the offer a second thought. But she's still considering it. This could be more serious than we think."

"I don't like the way you said that."

"I think it's time to increase our efforts," Jessica told her. "Why don't I make reservations at Tiberino's for them for tomorrow night?"

Elizabeth looked thoughtful. "OK. But if that doesn't work—"

"Huh?" Jessica said distractedly. "Oh, look, there's Lila," she said, waving across the cafeteria to her friend.

"Hi, guys," Lila said, putting down her tray. Coming out of the cafeteria line closely behind her was Caroline, who started for an empty table in the far corner. Lila spotted her. "Oh, Caroline," she shouted too loudly for anyone to ignore. "Come join us."

Caroline felt the blood drain from her face. She'd been trying to avoid Lila and Jessica since the day before, but now she had no choice but to sit down at the table with them. She'd run out of excuses. "I'm sick of cafeteria food," she grumbled.

"I'm surprised you've got any appetite with the party this Saturday and all," Jessica said. "Did you send Adam the bus ticket?"

"Sure," Caroline said, trying to recover her usual exuberance. "I spoke to him last night. He's really excited about coming." She looked nervously at Elizabeth as she spoke. Had Jessica told her about Adam's letters yet?

"That's great!" Lila cried. She turned to Jessica. "See, I knew he couldn't resist being the guest of honor at a party. What boy could?"

"Especially when it's one of your parties, right, Lila?" Jessica said, giggling.

"Tell me a little about your boyfriend, Caroline," Elizabeth said. "Jessica told me he was coming down this weekend. What's he like?"

Caroline looked embarrassed. She fiddled with her macaroni. "He's tall and really good looking," she began. The usual excitement was lacking in her voice.

"Oh, come on, Caroline, he's much more than that," Lila interjected. "Liz, you'd be interested in this. Adam writes the most romantic love letters in the world. Caroline, why don't you read one to her?"

"No, I couldn't," she began. "I—"

"What's the problem?" Lila asked. "Don't tell me you don't have any with you."

"Well, if you insist." Caroline dug into her pocketbook for one of the letters she'd told them she always carried around with her. "I haven't gotten any since I came back from the weekend. This one is from last week. I hope you're not sick of it already."

"How could we be sick of anything so romantic?" Jessica asked. "I know Liz will really appreciate this. She's so literary, you know. And she loves the romantic stuff, especially all those nineteenth-century masters."

Elizabeth looked at her sister, trying to figure out what was going on. Jessica was definitely up to something. She was sure of that. Her twin looked as if she was about to burst out

110

laughing. But Elizabeth couldn't see the joke. What was so funny about love letters?

Caroline didn't see any humor in the situation either, although Jessica's comments had made perfect sense to her. Nervously she began to read. "My Beloved Caroline, I was happy, so happy before. But I am happier and richer now. Caroline, no words will do, but there is life before us, and I will live and die with your beautiful vision comforting me, blessing me . . .' "

At once Elizabeth saw what was going on. *My God, that's Robert Browning*, she thought with a start. One glance at her twin's face told her that Jessica knew the source of the letter as well as she did. *But what about Caroline?* she wondered. Did Caroline realize her boyfriend had been plagiarizing his love letters?

As Caroline went on reading, Elizabeth's gentle gaze darkened. *I used that letter in my play*, she thought angrily. *No wonder Jess knows where it's from! She and Lila have set Caroline and me up. And as uncomfortable as I feel, poor Caroline . . .*

Caroline stopped reading.

"Is anything wrong?" Jessica asked innocently.

"Uh, no," Caroline said. "I-I just lost my place." She looked back down at the letter. " 'When I think of all you have been and are to me, the delicious feeling makes the paper words that come seem vainer than ever.

" 'I'll write tomorrow. Until then I am all yours. Adam.' "

Angry sparks shooting from her blue-green eyes, Elizabeth tried to catch Jessica's gaze. But Jessica refused to look at her. Instead, Jessica sensed this was a good moment to make her escape and bounced up from the table. "Sorry I've got to leave, but I forgot all about the meeting I have with Robin Wilson. I've got to talk to her about some new cheers. See you guys around." She hurried off.

Lila quickly made an excuse, too. "I've got the most awful headache ever. I'm going to the nurse's office to get some aspirin." With a cheerful wave, Lila grabbed her yogurt container and was off, leaving Elizabeth and Caroline alone.

*Jessica's really done me a favor this time*, Elizabeth thought wryly. Elizabeth didn't want to be the one to have to tell poor Caroline that her letters weren't what she thought they were. On the other hand she didn't feel she could just sit by and watch her be the butt of what had obviously become an inside joke between Jessica and Lila.

If Elizabeth was feeling bad about the situation, Caroline felt a lot worse. She'd been waiting for Elizabeth to expose her as a fraud. At first she'd thought she'd been perfectly safe digging up Robert Browning's letters and making them her own. But as soon as she found out what Elizabeth's play was about, she knew she was in terrible trouble. It had just been a question of time.

Caroline knew she had to confess the truth to Elizabeth, and as she thought about it she realized that maybe it wasn't such a bad idea to come clean to someone. She'd been up all night trying to figure how she was going to deal with the upcoming party. She knew she had to say something soon, before Saturday night, but she didn't know how to do it. Maybe Elizabeth could help.

Nervously she held out the letter to Elizabeth. "There's something I've got to tell you," she said. "Something I've been afraid to tell Jessica and Lila. It's about these letters. Adam didn't write them."

"I know," Elizabeth said. "Robert Browning did. But that's not such a big problem, is it? So what if Adam's not original? I don't think Jessica and Lila really care about that. The important thing's the sentiment. To be honest, I was afraid you thought he wrote them himself. But if it doesn't bother you—"

"Well, there's more to it than that," Caroline interrupted.

"Like what?"

Caroline looked furtively around the cafeteria.

She saw Cara and several of her sorority sisters eating lunch, talking, making jokes. Everything they did was so open, so honest, not like the lie she'd almost started believing herself. The whole school would be laughing at her once the truth about Adam came out. But she knew Elizabeth could be trusted to keep quiet. "I've got to talk to you, Liz, but now isn't really the time or the place. Can you meet me after school?"

"I'm kind of busy," Elizabeth said.

Caroline looked at her pleadingly. "Please, Liz, I wouldn't be asking you if it wasn't something really important. I really have to talk to you!"

Something about the urgency in Caroline's voice got to Elizabeth. She was afraid Caroline might be in some sort of trouble. "OK," she said reluctantly. "Meet me by my locker after the last bell."

Caroline was waiting for Elizabeth after school. "Can we go for a walk?" she asked nervously. "I don't really want to talk about this around here."

"OK, Caroline," Elizabeth said pleasantly, taking a few books out of her locker and following the redhead. Once they were outside, they walked for several minutes before Caroline spoke up.

"Oh, Liz, what am I going to do about the party Jessica and Lila are throwing this weekend? I can't go through with it!"

"Why not?" Elizabeth asked her. "Doesn't Adam want to come?"

"I don't know how I ever got myself into such a mess." Tears welled up in Caroline's eyes. "There is no Adam," she confessed. "I made him up."

"*What!*" Elizabeth exclaimed, staring at Caroline. "Why?"

Caroline brushed the tears from her eyes. "I don't know," she said softly. "I guess I just wanted to fit in. Every time I heard other girls talk about their boyfriends, I got so jealous I couldn't stand it. I wanted a boyfriend, too. I was so desperate, Liz. . . . I used to lie awake nights and think about what this perfect boy would be like. Then one day it just happened. I shared my fantasy boy with the other girls. Things just built up from there, and I came up with the letters. Then things really got out of hand."

Elizabeth sighed. "I'm sorry you've been so lonely," she said softly. "But maybe you could do something more constructive about it."

"What do you mean?" Caroline asked.

"Well, you could try to talk to people—*really* talk, not just gossip," Elizabeth said carefully.

"Most people are willing to give others a chance, if you only let them."

"But it was so much better for a while because of Adam," Caroline told her. "People were really paying attention to me. They really cared what I was up to. Now all that's over."

"Maybe you shouldn't worry who's paying attention to *you*," Elizabeth said quietly. "A good friend pays attention to other people. The rest just sort of follows."

With the back of her hand, Caroline wiped away the tears that were running down her face. "Oh, Liz, what am I going to do?"

Elizabeth put her arm around her. "There's only one thing you *can* do—tell the truth now. It's going to be embarrassing no matter what, but better now than later."

"What about your play?" Caroline's expression was one of fear. "You're not still going to read it, are you?"

"I *have* to," Elizabeth told her gently. "It's part of the rules. We each have to read our play this Friday night. It's the only way to compete," she explained.

"But once you read it everyone's going to know where the letters came from! Oh, Liz, you can't do that to me!"

Elizabeth sighed. *What about me?* she thought

angrily. She'd slaved over this play, and she'd really been looking forward to reading it.

On the other hand, Caroline seemed desperate. And Elizabeth hated to compound the girl's troubles, even if most of them were her own fault.

"Well, maybe I can submit the play without reading it," she said halfheartedly. "I'll see what I can do, Caroline."

"Oh, thank you, Liz," Caroline cried, giving Elizabeth a hug.

"But if I *don't* read the play, that's not going to help you out Saturday night," Elizabeth reminded her.

"I know," Caroline said miserably. "I've got a lot of thinking to do," she admitted. "And I think some of the things you've told me are going to be a big help."

"I hope so," Elizabeth said uneasily. Personally, she wasn't so sure. She couldn't imagine Caroline changing overnight, and unless a six-foot-two-inch boy just happened to fall into her arms, she was going to have a lot of explaining to do.

# Twelve

When Elizabeth got home, she found Jessica lying on a float in the Wakefields' swimming pool, looking as if she didn't have a care in the world. "Jessica, I've got to talk to you," she said, trying to remain calm.

Jessica opened one eye lazily, closed it again, and readjusted herself on the float without saying a word.

"Jess, didn't you hear me?" Elizabeth raised her voice.

"Relax, Liz," Jessica said. "Whatever you've got to tell me can wait. The sun won't. I want to be tan for Lila's party."

"Lila's party," Elizabeth said, "is exactly what I want to talk to you about."

"Really?" Jessica asked innocently. "What about?"

"I just had a long talk with Caroline," Elizabeth began.

"Any talk with Caroline is a long one," Jessica said. "Hey, what did you think of Adam's letters? That boy sure can write, can't he?"

Elizabeth took off her shoes and dangled her feet in the water. "Come off it, Jess, we both know where those letters came from. Now I know why you got so excited about my play the other night." She sighed. "And I thought you really liked it."

"I really do," Jessica insisted. "It's fabulous." Still facing the sun, she adjusted her bathing suit top. "But you have to admit it was a bit of a shock for me to hear the same words that Adam used in his letters. If there even is an Adam," she added with a smirk.

"What do you mean?" Elizabeth demanded.

"I don't think he exists. I think Caroline made him up."

"And you still invited him to a party?" Elizabeth cried.

"Lila did the inviting, not me. Though I may have pushed her a bit. It's the only way we're going to know for sure about Adam. Lila still believes he's real, but I'm more convinced than

119

ever he's not. It's going to be fun to see how Caroline gets out of this one." Jessica's voice was full of mischief.

"Jessica Wakefield, you're awful. If you're so sure Adam's a fake, why don't you come right out and say so to Caroline?"

"That would spoil all the fun," Jessica said, giggling. "Caroline has it coming to her anyway. I can't believe she tried to trick us! I'll admit it showed she's got more imagination than I ever gave her credit for, but that's about all. And if I came right out and called her bluff, that would be the end of it. No, she deserves a lesson, one that has to be taught in public, for everyone to see."

*Jessica's done it again*, Elizabeth thought. As much as she loved her sister, she couldn't stand this malicious streak in her. Elizabeth hated to see anyone cornered like this, even someone as hard to like as Caroline. "But what if Adam turns out to be real?" she asked slowly, a thought coming to her.

"Did Caroline tell you he was?" Jessica asked. "What did you talk about anyway?"

"She's very upset, Jess. She's embarrassed about the letters. She knows that I know that Adam didn't write them, and she's afraid if the word gets out, she'll look like a fool."

Jessica looked up. Shading her eyes from the sun, she squinted in Elizabeth's direction. "The letters are all she's worried about?"

Elizabeth nodded. "She knows about my play, too, and asked me to cancel the reading."

"And you told her you'd do that?"

"Sort of," Elizabeth admitted.

Jessica nearly tipped over the float. "I thought you were the brains of the family, Liz, but that's about the dumbest thing you've ever done in your whole life. I can't believe you'd jeopardize your entire literary future for that spoiled brat."

"It's only a play," Elizabeth rationalized. "There'll be others." She looked down into the water. "I just couldn't say no to her."

"So she roped you into her scheme. Do yourself a favor and forget you ever said yes."

"I felt so bad for her."

"She's brought it on herself," Jessica said angrily. "She doesn't deserve your sympathy. Not to mention your sacrifices."

"I'll think about it," Elizabeth said.

"I'm serious, Liz. That girl never did anything for you."

Elizabeth shrugged. Jessica had a point, but she still didn't like the way her twin had been treating Caroline. Something had just occurred to her, and she jumped to her feet. "I've got to call Todd," she said, hurrying inside and leaving Jessica staring after her. *Todd'll know how to help me with this one,* she added silently. *It's a tall order—about six feet two.* She chuckled. *But I have a feeling it may help teach that twin of mine a lesson!*

Caroline was lying on her bed reading when Anita dropped in on her later that evening. "Another letter from Adam?"

"No, just going over my history notes," Caroline said, putting down her notebook. "Will you help me with my hair again tonight?"

Anita looked really apologetic. "I can't tonight. I just came in to see if you got any more letters."

"No, I haven't heard from him in several days." Caroline's admission was barely louder than a whisper.

Anita sat down on the edge of the bed. "That's a shame. I hope you're not having problems."

"Oh, it's nothing like that. Why'd you ask, anyway?"

"I was just wondering what's going on with you two."

Caroline froze momentarily. "N-nothing."

"No? Then why are you hiding him from Mom? I just happened to mention him to her now, and she told me she'd never heard of him. Why haven't you told her?"

Caroline felt her world collapsing around her.

For a long time she just sat and looked at her bedspread, counting the stripes in the plaid pattern. She wanted to blurt out another excuse, just to get rid of her sister, but she couldn't make the words come out.

The only thing she could think of was the truth. "Anita, I don't have a boyfriend named Adam. I made him up, and I made up the letters."

At first Anita did nothing but stare at her sister in disbelief. "Why, Caroline?" she managed finally. "Why would you do a thing like that?"

Caroline burst into tears. "Because I was lonely!" she retorted. "I was sick and tired of being a misfit, that's why! Don't you realize how rough it's been for me, watching you go out with boys all the time? I wanted to know what it was like. I'll never find a real boy who'll like me!"

"Oh, Caroline," Anita cried, putting her arms around her sister. "Of course you will! But not *this* way," she admonished. "You know something? I think it's about time you and I had a good long talk. OK?"

Caroline nodded. "I need your help," she admitted. "Do you really think there's hope left for me?"

Anita started to laugh. "I'd say so. If you're really ready to listen, that is."

Caroline smiled through her tears. "I *am* ready," she promised.

And for the first time in her life, Caroline really *did* listen. For the next two hours she sat perfectly still, interrupting Anita only to ask a question now and then. Without flinching she heard all the hurtful things Anita had to say about Caroline's behavior at school. Anita was right, and Caroline knew it. But she was ready to change, and she wanted every bit of advice Anita could offer.

"The point is," Anita concluded, "that you have to *listen* to other people and really think before you say anything. You have to ask yourself if what you're about to say is going to make them feel better. If it hurts *anyone*, it's not worth saying."

*Like Annie and Ricky*, Caroline thought, biting her lip. *Or telling Elizabeth about Bill Chase and Mr. Jaworski. Or telling Lila that John Pfeifer had gotten thrown off the paper.*

"Liz told me the same thing," Caroline said gratefully, giving Anita a hug. "And I think I'm finally ready to do something about it now. Anita, how can I ever thank you enough?"

"Just be yourself," Anita told her, hugging her back. "And don't worry about that party, either," she warned. "Together we'll make sure you look absolutely gorgeous. And you'll just have to hold your head high and show Jessica and Lila they can't get to you."

Taking a deep breath, Caroline nodded. She wasn't sure what she was going to do next. But one thing was obvious—she was going to have to change. And the time to start was that moment.

The next morning Caroline found Elizabeth at her locker. "I've been doing a lot of thinking," she said. "I can't let you cancel your play reading."

"Are you sure? I don't want to cause problems for you," Elizabeth said.

Caroline was amazed, and very ashamed of herself. Never in her life had she been that selfless. Never, that is, until now. "No, it's not fair for me to make you do that," she said. "I never should have asked you in the first place. I should have realized if you went to all the trouble of researching Browning's letters that this play must mean an awful lot to you. But I wasn't thinking of you—only of me. You shouldn't have to make that kind of sacrifice for me."

"Thanks, Caroline. I appreciate it," Elizabeth said with great relief. "But what are you going to do about Adam?"

"What I should have done a long time ago. Tell the truth. I'm going to find Jessica and Lila and tell them now."

Elizabeth looked down the hallway. "I don't think you're going to have to search far. Here they come."

Caroline tensed up. This was the moment she knew she was going to have to face. But she'd hoped it wouldn't come so soon. Right now she wished she could climb into Elizabeth's locker and hide. Instead, she summoned up all her inner courage. "Lila, Jessica," she called. "Got a minute?"

Curious, Lila and Jessica came over to her. Jessica felt it was more than coincidence that her sister was standing next to Caroline, her face full of concern. "Do you have something to tell us?" she asked. Then she turned to Elizabeth and winked as if she already knew the answer.

"As a matter of fact I do," Caroline said haltingly. "It's, um, about Adam."

"I thought so." Jessica said complacently. She nudged Lila. "Does it have to do with the party?"

"The party?" Caroline felt her courage start to flag. "Uh, not exactly. But there's something I've got to tell you. It's—it's about the letters. His letters. Though they're not exactly his letters.

I mean they are his letters, but he didn't write them—"

"I'm getting confused," Lila interrupted.

"What I'm trying to say is that Adam didn't write the letters. They were copied out of a book. That great romantic stuff was Robert Browning's, not Adam's. All he did was change around some of the words."

Clearly this wasn't what Jessica had expected to hear. "But he sent you the letters?"

Caroline nodded, ignoring the awful feeling in the pit of her stomach. Faced with this formidable duo, all of her earlier intentions to confess had dissolved. She couldn't bear to have them laugh at her. "I'm a little embarrassed after the way I built him up for you. I guess he's not such a great poet after all." She felt as if she were about to cry.

"Hey, what's with the sad face?" Lila asked, putting an arm around Caroline. "A guy wouldn't go to all that trouble if he didn't care about you."

"That's true," Caroline agreed. "I just wanted to get this into the open, with Elizabeth's play coming up and all. I didn't want anyone jumping to any conclusions."

"I'm still looking forward to meeting him," Lila said. "He *is* coming to the party, isn't he?"

"Oh, yes," Caroline blurted out, her courage completely gone. "He'll be there."

After Jessica and Lila left, Caroline begged Elizabeth for her forgiveness. "Don't worry, Liz, go ahead with your play as scheduled. I swear I'll tell them the truth before Saturday. I swear it!"

But Elizabeth wasn't so sure. All morning long she couldn't get Caroline out of her mind. She truly felt sorry for her now. She understood why Caroline had done it, how her loneliness had gotten to be more than she could take. She wished she could do something to help her. And she knew that at this point even canceling her play reading wouldn't be enough.

At lunch she confided her feelings to Todd. "Caroline may not be the most likable person in the world, but that's because she's been going about everything the wrong way. Basically she's like everyone else. She deserves some happiness, too."

Todd didn't quite believe his ears. "Something must have happened for you to say that."

"I think something has, Todd. I think this whole experience has made Caroline realize you can't win friends by deception. She seemed different to me this morning, more willing to give of herself than ever before. She didn't have to ask me not to cancel the play reading, and after the way she practically begged me yesterday, it really surprised me."

"So, you'd still like to get her out of the mess she created for herself?"

"Something like that." Elizabeth smiled. "It would just *kill* Jessica," she added.

Todd pursed his lips. "OK," he said, grinning. "We go ahead with Operation Rescue."

Elizabeth's eyes lit up. "I knew I could count on you."

Todd held up his hands. "Hey, wait a second. Not so fast. This plan may take a few days to put together. Don't thank me yet. Not until Saturday night."

Caroline carried her tray to the table where Bill Chase and DeeDee Gordon were sitting. "The table's full," DeeDee said, her voice icy.

"I don't want to stay," Caroline said. "I'll make this quick. I came to apologize to you, Bill. I was the one who spread the rumor about your cheating on the play contest."

DeeDee put down her sandwich in shock. "You're actually admitting it?"

"It was a dumb thing for me to do. I know it. I've said a lot of dumb things lately, and I'm really sorry about it. I hope it didn't upset you too much."

"You know he's not competing in the contest now," DeeDee said.

"Oh, no!" Caroline cried. "Oh, Bill, if there's anything I can do . . ."

"That won't be necessary," Bill said. He started to smile. "DeeDee's just giving you a hard time. The real reason why I dropped out of the competition has nothing to do with you. See, you got half the story right. You saw me taking books from Mr. Jaworski, but you didn't know why. He was giving me material for an audition I had yesterday with some producers from Los Angeles. They liked it, and now they've called me in for a taping next week."

"That's wonderful!" Caroline cried. "And don't worry, I'll keep my mouth shut if you want me to."

"That's OK, you can tell anyone you want. This is really happening," he said. "If they like what they see, I could end up in a TV series."

"I'm really happy for you," Caroline said.

"But don't go around telling everyone I'm already a star," Bill warned. "I've got a lot of hard work ahead of me—and it's not guaranteed anyway."

"My days of spreading rumors are over," Caroline declared. "I see now that I've caused nothing but trouble, for myself as well as everyone else."

130

And for the first time, Caroline actually felt better about the whole mess she'd made. *I know I can't expect miraculous changes overnight*, she told herself. *But it sure feels good to have made a start!*

# Thirteen

"I didn't think you two would still be up," Mrs. Wakefield said, coming into the living room and taking off her coat.

"How was Tiberino's?" Jessica asked. "Was Sal there? Did you have lasagna?"

"It was fabulous," Mr. Wakefield admitted, putting his arm around his wife. "What are you two watching? It looks awful," he complained, squinting at the television.

"A rerun of 'The Streets of San Francisco,' " Elizabeth said solemnly. "It's really violent tonight," she added.

Mrs. Wakefield laughed. "Enough!" she burst out. "I think it's time to tell them, Ned. They've been patient enough as it is."

132

"Go ahead," he said.

Alice Wakefield sat down and leaned toward the girls. "No one's leaving Sweet Valley—at least not for the time being. I decided not to accept that job offer."

"Oh, Mom," Elizabeth cried. "You didn't have to do that for us."

"Shut up, dummy," Jessica hissed at her sister. "We're staying!" Turning back to her mother, she said, "That's great!"

"But I may accept it in the future. When I sat down to analyze the situation, I realized I had too much to lose by leaving right now. And it wouldn't be fair to uproot you in your junior year of high school. When I explained the situation to Mr. Paine last week, he told me they'd have a spot for me whenever I'm ready to make the move."

"Last week?" Elizabeth and Jessica cried at the same time. "Why did you wait until now to tell us?" Jessica added.

Mr. Wakefield smiled. "It was my idea not to tell you sooner. I was upset about the way you girls treated your mother. I wanted to wait a day or so before telling you. It was my way of punishing you for not giving your mother the consideration she deserves."

"But then you started your public relations campaign on Sweet Valley, and we got so caught up in it we decided to let it continue, to see where you took it," their mother added.

"You lied to us!" Jessica said. "That day I got you out to Las Palmas Canyon—you already knew then, didn't you, Daddy?"

"Yes, but I didn't lie. I just held out on the truth a little," Mr. Wakefield said. "I have to admit I liked the attention I was getting."

"So did I," Mrs. Wakefield agreed. "It wasn't such a bad thing, as I look back on it. You girls helped me to rediscover places I'd forgotten. I even found some new ones I didn't know about. Those brochures you had mailed to us were very helpful. And Tiberino's was fabulous! But enough is enough. I didn't want you to think we'd hold out on you forever."

"Thank goodness," Elizabeth said. "Now I can stop worrying about moving and start worrying about the play competition." She could hardly wait to run upstairs and call Todd to tell him the wonderful news. The Wakefields were staying in Sweet Valley.

The lights went up in the auditorium as Elizabeth read the last line of her play and closed her notebook, her heart hammering in her chest. A minute later, the audience burst into wild applause. The hush that followed her final words filled Elizabeth with joy. It showed she had

134

moved the audience, had managed to convey something of the bittersweet romance to her listeners. But what would the judges think?

"That was fabulous," Todd whispered, squeezing her hand as she took her seat. Elizabeth shook her head. "I've still got some stiff competition," she told him. Bill Chase was no longer in the running, but several other juniors had submitted entries. And each of them seemed awfully good to Elizabeth. She could barely believe it when the head judge, Mr. Jaworski, called her name.

"And the winner," he announced, "is Elizabeth Wakefield's *One Woman's Romance*. Elizabeth, could you come up here, please?"

Heart pounding, Elizabeth went up to the front of the auditorium to accept her trophy. The applause that followed Mr. Jaworski's announcement was deafening.

"I'm so happy," Elizabeth whispered to Todd as they left the auditorium some time later. "Do you think I sounded all right?"

"You were superb," Todd assured her.

"Liz?" A shy voice asked. Caroline Pearce came forward and wrapped Elizabeth in a warm embrace. "Congratulations," she said warmly. "I'm so proud of you."

"Thanks, Caroline," Elizabeth said happily.

Todd had dropped back to talk to one of his friends, leaving her alone with Caroline.

"I thought the play was beautiful," Caroline added. "You really brought both of those characters to life. I thought it might be hard to listen to those letters," she admitted, "but instead it made me feel much better. I guess I saw how constructive creating a character can be when the circumstances are right."

Elizabeth smiled at her sympathetically. "Have you told anyone about Adam yet?"

Caroline stared at the floor. "No, not yet," she admitted, "but I will."

Elizabeth sighed. "But the party's tomorrow night!"

"Don't I know that! I've hardly slept in days, worrying about this. But every time I try to open my mouth and tell the truth, I chicken out. I guess I'm just going to wait until the party. I won't have a choice then."

"Actually, that's a good idea," Elizabeth said thoughtfully. "It might be better for you to make an announcement to everyone and get it over with all at once."

"I'm scared, Liz. I know I brought this on myself, but the idea of telling everyone I'm a liar is just awful."

"I can understand that, but it might not be as bad as you think."

136

"How could you say that?"

"All I can say is trust me, Caroline. Very often the things you fear most are things that end up turning out all right at the end. Call it a gut feeling or an intuition, but I think everything is going to work out for you."

"I wish I had your confidence," Caroline said.

"You will if you just go to the party in as positive a frame of mind as you can."

"Anita's taking me to Lisette's to look for a new dress," Caroline admitted shyly. "And she's going to fix my hair, too. Maybe that'll help."

"I'm sure it will," Elizabeth said, giving Caroline an impulsive hug. "I'll be rooting for you," she whispered. And she really meant it, too. Everything had worked out so well for *her*—she'd won the play competition, and she didn't have to leave Sweet Valley. Now Elizabeth wanted to do what she could to come to Caroline's rescue.

When Elizabeth and Todd met Caroline outside the gates of Fowler Crest the following evening, Elizabeth could barely believe her eyes. Caroline looked beautiful. She was wearing a flattering new green satin dress, and Anita had brushed her hair back with tortoiseshell combs. Her eyes looked bigger than usual, thanks to a bit of green shadow lining her lashes.

But what really made the difference was Caroline's expression. However nervous she felt, she looked perfectly composed. *She looks almost regal*, Elizabeth thought appreciatively. *As if she can handle anything tonight—even my twin sister*.

"Wow," was all Todd could say. "Is that really you?"

Caroline smiled shyly. "Do I really look nice?"

"Yeah. There's something different about you tonight—and it's not just your new dress. You're pretty," he said.

"Thanks. I always wanted to look nice for my funeral," Caroline joked.

"Hey, that's no way to talk," Elizabeth said. "Remember—confidence!"

Caroline gulped. "It's going to take a miracle for me to get through this." Caroline bit her lip as they passed through the tall iron gates leading to the Spanish-style house. *This is it*, she thought as Todd rang the doorbell.

There was no turning back now. One of the Fowler servants greeted them, ushering them into the majestic foyer. The party was already in full swing, and Caroline could hear the loud, driving music coming from the back of the house.

The realization that time had run out had a funny effect on Caroline. Holding her head high, she walked on ahead of Elizabeth and Todd through the long corridor that led to the back lawn, where the party was being held.

Lila had spared no expense for the gathering. Several long, rectangular tables set up on the patio were heaped with platters of food, and there were enough bottles of soda to quench the thirst of the entire town. Lila had even hired a mobile disco for the occasion. Two large portable monitors were hooked up at one end of the large patio, playing rock videos, the sound cranked up high enough to echo into the valley below them. A few couples were already dancing, while others were standing around and talking next to the Fowlers' Olympic-sized pool.

Caroline passed by the food and went straight up to Lila, who was talking with friends at one of the poolside tables. "Hello, Lila," she said. "The place looks gorgeous!"

Lila almost didn't recognize the girl standing before her. It took a moment for her to recover. "Well, well, the guest of honor is here." She looked around her now. "Or is he? Where's Adam?"

"Yes, Adam." She hesitated. *Don't lose it now,* Caroline told herself. "There's something I've got to tell you about him. Has Jessica gotten here yet?"

"I think she's holding court over by the pool," Lila said, pointing in that direction.

"Good," said Caroline. "Could you turn down the music? I've got an announcement to make. And I want everyone to hear it."

# Fourteen

With the music off, the grounds of Fowler Crest were eerily silent. Everyone there sensed something important was about to happen and began to congregate on the patio. Jessica, too, walked over, realizing that the moment she'd been waiting for was upon them.

The great fall of Caroline Pearce.

Lila rapped her fist on one of the tables. "Attention everyone. Caroline has just told me that she has an announcement to make."

Todd checked his watch and looked helplessly at Elizabeth. She held her breath and watched sadly as Caroline turned to face the crowd.

Still holding her head up, the petrified girl

stood alone before her classmates. Their eyes stared back at her in anticipation, and at that moment Caroline knew the meaning of the word *fear*. Those eyes were demanding, accusing, and getting increasingly impatient with each passing second. She had to get this over with, if for no other reason than to get those eyes off her. "Thanks for coming tonight," she began. "I know you all came here to meet the boy I've been telling you so much about, but he—"

"Caroline!" A boy's voice cut through her words, and she was struck mute as a tall, friendly looking boy rushed up and gave her a big hug. "Sorry I'm late. I hope you'll forgive me."

Caroline felt like shouting "Who are you?" But the boy quieted the impulse with a kiss.

"Tell them who I am," he whispered while their lips were still pressed together.

She regained her composure quickly. Without even thinking about it she announced, "As I was saying, everybody, here's Adam!"

"That's him?" Jessica's jaw dropped.

"Of course, dummy," Lila said smugly. "He looks just like his picture, don't you think?"

The boy did fit the description Caroline had painted: six feet two, dark hair, with a strong, muscular build. His features weren't quite up to pinup quality, but Caroline could be forgiven for that exaggeration. By anyone's standards he was a winner.

"I just don't believe it," Jessica said, slumping into the nearest chair. "She must have pulled him out of a hat."

"Come on, Jess, face it. When you're wrong, you're wrong." Lila smiled. "I knew all along he'd show up." She watched as he took Caroline's arm and walked her toward the pool. "Caroline is some lucky girl."

Once she was sure they were out of earshot, Caroline stopped and looked up at her savior. "Who are you?" she asked.

"Adam," he said.

"Please don't joke with me. I'm serious."

He smiled. "I was told that was who I was supposed to be. Actually my name is Jerry Fisher. I'm a friend of Todd Wilkins's."

"Todd's?" A light went on in Caroline's head as she realized now what Elizabeth had meant about things having a way of working out. "I'm very grateful to you, Jerry. You just saved my life."

"Todd told me what happened. I'm happy to help out. He's a good friend of mine."

"And mine, too, I realize now. I'm very lucky to have such good friends, especially after the way I've been acting. You're a terrific person to want to help pull off a dumb stunt like this."

143

"I'm happy to play Adam for the night. Just don't ask me to recite poetry." He winked. "I can't stand the stuff."

Caroline laughed. "That's OK, but I hope you know something about baseball. I told everyone that Adam played."

"No problem there," Jerry said. "I play for Woodgrove High. I also play basketball, which is how I first met Todd. Speaking of which, I see him dancing over there with Elizabeth. Want to join them?"

In a daze, Caroline followed Jerry to the dance area. Everything had happened so quickly she was only now trying to make sense of it. All she knew was that Elizabeth and Todd had gotten her out of the biggest jam of her life, and as far as everyone there was concerned, Adam was exactly as she'd portrayed him.

Everything was working out perfectly. She couldn't ask for anything more.

On the dance floor Caroline thanked Elizabeth and Todd for their help. "I don't know what else to say but thank you—from the bottom of my heart," she told them. "You didn't have to do this for me."

"We wanted to help," Elizabeth said. "And as long as you have a good time tonight, that's all that matters."

Caroline had more than a good time. Jerry,

alias Adam, stuck to her side the entire night. He entertained her with real baseball stories and told her what it was like to live in Woodgrove, a small town up in the mountains, about an hour's drive away. Caroline listened attentively, and for the first time in her life she didn't have the urge to interrupt with some fact about herself. On the contrary, she didn't feel like talking about herself at all.

It was wonderful to be the center of a boy's attention, she realized, even if it was all an act. Caroline was especially pleased when Lila sidled up to Jerry and asked him to dance with her, and he declined politely. "I'm a one-woman guy," he explained.

"You didn't have to do that," Caroline chided him, though inside she felt the satisfaction of having beaten a rival. "Lila is the hostess, after all."

"Not on your life. I'm here to spend the evening with *you*," Jerry said warmly.

But despite herself, Caroline began to feel uneasy. She was having a wonderful time with Jerry, yet she could never for a moment forget it was all a game. He was only playing a role, just like the one she was playing by pretending to everyone that he was someone else.

As the hours passed, she felt less and less smug about having pulled a fast one on everyone. There was no satisfaction in that. While everyone else was thinking how wonderful it was for her to have Adam, she knew the truth, that she was as lonely as she had ever been. And after that evening, when Jerry went back to Woodgrove, she'd still have to make up new stories about Adam. Everybody would be asking when he'd be coming down, and sooner or later she'd have to make him materialize again.

She knew she could never ask Jerry to do that. She was even starting to feel bad about his being there that night. He had no business participating in her crazy deception.

Finally she couldn't take it any longer. Realizing her conscience wouldn't rest, she asked Lila again to turn down the music.

This time she felt calmer, steeled by the confidence she felt in knowing that at long last she was doing the right thing. "I've got another announcement to make," she told the group. "I'll try to make it brief and simple. I wanted to be like all of you. I wanted to have a boyfriend, to feel as if I belonged with everyone here. When I couldn't get one on my own, I did the next best thing. I made one up. There is no Adam. This nice guy"—she pointed to Jerry—"is playing a role. He wanted to help out so I wouldn't look like a fool in front of you. But I feel foolish anyway. I just wanted to let you know."

Caroline ran off toward the back part of the sloping lawn, where it was dark. She hadn't wanted to cry, hadn't thought she would, but now the tears were flowing freely and making the world ahead blur. Although it had felt good to get the truth out into the open, the empty feeling still remained. As she fell onto the soft grass, she wondered whether she'd ever be able to face anyone again.

Suddenly she felt a hand on her shoulder. "I'm very proud of you, Caroline," Jerry said. He sat down next to her.

She looked up at him. "You are? But you don't even know me."

He smiled warmly and brushed away the tears from her cheek. "Sure I do. I've had all night to get to know you. It takes a lot of guts to do what you just did. Most people I know would have just kept quiet."

"I couldn't," Caroline said. "I was tired of living a lie. I hope I didn't embarrass you."

"I don't think you could."

"Everybody must think I'm a fool now."

Jerry shook his head. "I don't think so. Didn't you see the looks on their faces when you told them the truth? I guess there were a couple who laughed, but what I saw mostly was respect.

147

Everybody's done something at one time or another that they'd rather not own up to. But it takes a big person to admit they've done wrong. I'm glad I got to see that part of you."

"I'm grateful for your sympathy."

"Hey, it's not that at all. I'm really having a good time with you tonight. I'll admit I didn't expect much when Todd asked me to come, but you're all right. I like you."

"You do?" Caroline was doubtful. No boy had ever said that to her before.

"Don't look at me like I'm crazy. It's not crazy to like you, is it?"

Caroline paused before answering. "No, I guess not," she said, starting to smile.

"Then there's something I'd like to ask you. I'm going to have to be leaving soon, but I'd like to get to know you better. Would you mind if I wrote to you?"

"I'd love that, Jerry," Caroline said sincerely. "And I promise I'll never read your letters to anyone. Do you think I could even come up and visit you in Woodgrove some time?"

"I'd like that, too." As proof, he held her in his arms and kissed her, not as Adam but as Jerry, a slightly less than perfect boy, but one more wonderful than anyone Caroline could have imagined.

\*   \*   \*

"Well, well, well," Lila said, smiling archly at Jessica as she lifted her soda. "I guess things didn't turn out so badly for poor Caroline after all."

Jessica flushed. She had to admit she hadn't enjoyed this evening half as much as she'd expected to. Not even Caroline's public confession had been very satisfying. And now Caroline was dancing with this mysterious guy, whoever he was.

"Never mind," she said. "Who cares about Caroline Pearce anyway? I've got better things to think about."

*I'll bet you have*, Lila thought slyly, watching Jessica walk off. *I'll just bet!*

"I told her things had a way of working out," Elizabeth said to Todd. From their vantage point on the patio, they had a clear view of Caroline and Jerry. "I'm glad she got everything out in the open. Life's complicated enough without having to spend half your time covering your tracks."

"I like having things out in the open, too," Todd said, slipping an arm around Elizabeth's waist. "Like knowing you don't have to move to San Francisco, for example." He followed with a deep and lingering kiss.

"Wow, I didn't expect that," Elizabeth whispered.

"It must be something in the air." Todd waved his arm. A number of couples had slipped off into the darkness to be alone together.

Elizabeth's eyes lit on one particular couple near the pool house. "I don't like the looks of that," she said, frowning. She pointed to Bruce, holding Regina in his arms.

"I thought you were all in favor of love," Todd said.

"Love, yes, but not what Bruce is up to. I don't think he knows what love means. All he knows is what makes him feel good."

"Regina doesn't seem to be complaining."

"She thinks he really cares for her. And she's completely fallen for him. I just wish there were some way I could protect her from him!"

Todd smiled. He knew his girlfriend too well and realized that she wouldn't give up until she got through to Regina. "If anyone can come to the rescue, I have a feeling it's you," he said lightly, drawing her back in his arms.

Elizabeth eyed the couple over his shoulder, shaking her head with concern. "I wish I could think so," she murmured. "But I have a feeling Regina Morrow may be in for big trouble!"

*Will loving Bruce bring Regina happiness or heartache? Find out in Sweet Valley High #18,* **HEAD OVER HEELS.**

# SWEET VALLEY HIGH

| | | | |
|---|---|---|---|
| ☐ | 26682 | RUNAWAY #21 | $2.75 |
| ☐ | 26745 | TOO MUCH IN LOVE #22 | $2.75 |
| ☐ | 26689 | SAY GOODBYE #23 | $2.75 |
| ☐ | 26684 | MEMORIES #24 | $2.75 |
| ☐ | 26748 | NOWHERE TO RUN #25 | $2.75 |
| ☐ | 26749 | HOSTAGE! #26 | $2.75 |
| ☐ | 26750 | LOVESTRUCK #27 | $2.75 |
| ☐ | 26825 | ALONE IN THE CROWD #28 | $2.75 |
| ☐ | 25728 | BITTER RIVALS #29 | $2.50 |
| ☐ | 25816 | JEALOUS LIES #30 | $2.50 |
| ☐ | 25886 | TAKING SIDES #31 | $2.75 |
| ☐ | 26113 | THE NEW JESSICA #32 | $2.75 |
| ☐ | 26198 | STARTING OVER #33 | $2.75 |
| ☐ | 26294 | FORBIDDEN LOVE #34 | $2.75 |
| ☐ | 26341 | OUT OF CONTROL #35 | $2.75 |
| ☐ | 26478 | LAST CHANCE #36 | $2.75 |
| ☐ | 26530 | RUMORS #37 | $2.75 |
| ☐ | 26568 | LEAVING HOME #38 | $2.75 |
| ☐ | 26673 | SECRET ADMIRER #39 | $2.75 |
| ☐ | 26703 | ON THE EDGE #40 | $2.75 |
| ☐ | 26866 | OUTCAST #41 | $2.75 |

**Prices and availability subject to change without notice.**

Buy them at your local bookstore or use this convenient coupon for ordering:

**SWEET DREAMS** are fresh, fun and exciting—alive with the flavor of the contemporary teen scene—the joy and doubt of *first love*. If you've missed any SWEET DREAMS titles, then you're missing out on *your* kind of stories, written about people like *you*!

| | | | |
|---|---|---|---|
| ☐ | 25814 | PRIVATE EYES #113<br>Julia Winfield | $2.50 |
| ☐ | 25815 | JUST THE WAY YOU ARE #114<br>Janice Boies | $2.50 |
| ☐ | 26158 | PROMISE ME LOVE #115<br>Jane Redish | $2.50 |
| ☐ | 26195 | HEARTBREAK HILL #116<br>Carol MacBain | $2.50 |
| ☐ | 26196 | THE OTHER ME #117<br>Terri Fields | $2.50 |
| ☐ | 26293 | HEART TO HEART #118<br>Stefanie Curtis | $2.50 |
| ☐ | 26339 | STAR-CROSSED LOVE #119<br>Sharon Cadwallader | $2.50 |
| ☐ | 26340 | MR. WONDERFUL #120<br>Fran Michaels | $2.50 |
| ☐ | 26418 | ONLY MAKE-BELIEVE #121<br>Julia Winfield | $2.50 |
| ☐ | 26419 | STARS IN HER EYES #122<br>Dee Daley | $2.50 |
| ☐ | 26481 | LOVE IN THE WINGS #123<br>Virginia Smiley | $2.50 |
| ☐ | 26482 | MORE THAN FRIENDS #124<br>Janice Boies | $2.50 |
| ☐ | 26528 | PARADE OF HEARTS #125<br>Cloverdale Press | $2.50 |
| ☐ | 26566 | HERE'S MY HEART #126<br>Stefanie Curtis | $2.50 |
| ☐ | 26567 | MY BEST ENEMY #127<br>Janet Quin-Harkin | $2.50 |
| ☐ | 26671 | ONE BOY AT A TIME #128<br>Diana Gregory | $2.50 |
| ☐ | 26672 | A VOTE FOR LOVE #129<br>Terri Fields | $2.50 |
| ☐ | 26701 | DANCE WITH ME #130<br>Jahnna Beecham | $2.50 |
| ☐ | 26865 | HAND-ME-DOWN HEART #131<br>Mary Schultz | $2.50 |
| ☐ | 26790 | WINNER TAKES ALL #132<br>Laurie Lykken | $2.50 |
| ☐ | 26864 | PLAYING THE FIELD #133<br>Eileen Hehl | $2.50 |
| ☐ | 26789 | PAST PERFECT #134<br>Fran Michaels | $2.50 |

### Prices and availability subject to change without notice.

# BANTAM
## SHOP·AT·HOME
### C·A·T·A·L·O·G

# Special Offer
# Buy a Bantam Book
# *for only 50¢.*

Now you can order the exciting books you've been wanting to read straight from Bantam's latest catalog of hundreds of titles. *And* this special offer gives you the opportunity to purchase a Bantam book for only 50¢. Here's how:

By ordering any five books at the regular price per order, you can also choose any other single book listed (up to a $5.95 value) for only 50¢. Some restrictions do apply, so for further details send for Bantam's catalog of titles today.

Just send us your name and address and we'll send you Bantam Book's SHOP AT HOME CATALOG!